Matchmakers
By Bernadette Marie

5 PRINCE PUBLISHING AND BOOKS, LLC
PO Box 16507
Denver, CO 80216
www.5PrinceBooks.com

ISBN 13:9781631120183 ISBN 10: 1631120182
Matchmakers
Bernadette Marie
Copyright AUTHOR 2013
Published by 5 Prince Publishing

Front Cover Viola Estrella

Third Edition February 2014 U.S.A.

5 PRINCE PUBLISHING AND BOOKS, LLC.

To Stan
When my belief in myself falters, yours never does.
Thank you!
I love you!

Acknowledgements

To my true love:
There will always be a first copy for you!

To my 5 Princes:
I will never forget your pride in this book. You showed it off, you hyped it up, you screamed when I opened the box. I'm so glad it is home with me again and I'm glad you've always been excited to see me grow as an author.

To my mom, dad, and sissy:
Thank you for wishing good things for me.
My book is home.

To Susan:
I could write a book about what we went through to get this book back with us. You have been such an inspiration, a teacher, a friend, and a pillar of support for me
all these years. Thank you.

To Connie and Marie:
Again, how could I ever get it all done without you? Thank you for falling into my life!

To Anne:
You make me look good lady!

To the original Warrior Princesses:
Antoinette, Adrienne, Gillian, Alexa, and Chris
Thank you for taking this and making me realize I had what it took! Your words to me made it possible and I knew I could accomplish what I now have. Your love and support will forever mean everything to me.

Dear Reader,

Matchmakers has taken quite a journey to end up where it is today. This book was my first contracted book, my pride and joy, my baby. After years, it is back home with me and available in its new rereleased state with 5 Prince Publishing.

I hope you enjoy the story of Sophia Burkhalter, the world renowned cellist, and her true love, David Kendal. And what would a true love story be if there wasn't a little teenage drama added in, courtesy of David's daughter Carissa.

I was so blessed when I first wrote this book that the early readers wanted more. They wanted a story for each of the charismatic women you meet in this book. *Encore* and *Finding Hope* encompass those asked for stories in books two and three of the Matchmaker series.

Enjoy *Matchmakers,* and here's to Happily Ever After!

Happy Reading!
Bernadette Marie

Matchmakers

CHAPTER ONE

Sophia filed off the airplane along with the other groggy passengers. The red-eye flight to Kansas City had knotted up her stomach. What in the hell was she doing back here?

Perfect persuasion and just the right amount of guilt had gotten her on that plane. Perhaps the tightening of her stomach wasn't the flying—it could very well be that she'd returned to the very place she'd run from ten years ago.

She'd run from a man and shattered the hearts of people she loved. The guilt stung a little deeper. She should have come home years earlier.

Sophia followed a small group of women from the plane into the ladies' room. Exhaustion weighed down her shoulders. Within the hour, she'd be at her grandmother's house, tucked into her childhood bed, and asleep. In the meantime, she splashed cool water on her face to keep herself alert.

She dried her face and hands and adjusted the scarf at her neck to ensure it hid the secret she kept from the world. She picked up the carry-on luggage at her feet and headed toward baggage claim.

"Sophia."

The husky voice was soft and male and made her knees weak when she heard it. She knew that voice as well as she knew her own. The knot in her stomach returned, but this time it was like a fist in her gut.

She turned to see him standing there in his pilot's uniform with his suitcase at his side—David Kendal, the very man she'd run from so many years ago.

He took his pilot's hat off and revealed the dark, wavy hair that she'd once run her fingers through. It was now speckled with hints of sophisticated silver. His uniform was striking on him—just as it had always been. Even in the early morning hour, she felt her skin tingle when she looked at his broad shoulders and knew what it was like to rest her head against his chest.

"David." His name floated from her lips in a sigh. Ten years had passed since she'd last laid eyes on him, and now he was as large as life standing before her.

"I thought that was you on the plane." He was walking closer to her, and her trembling knees wouldn't allow her to run the other direction.

The scent of his cologne washed over her. His dark eyes were smoky and wide as she watched him take in the sight of her.

"You look wonderful." He stepped closer, and Sophia gripped her bag tighter and tried to swallow the ball of fear that had lodged in her throat. He gripped his hat tighter. "I've been following your career."

"Really?" The muscles in her shoulders tensed. "Why?"

"Why?" He chuckled and took one more step closer, and her throat constricted. "Sophia, you're…" He shrugged as though brushing off a thought. "You're very talented."

Sophia shook her head, trying desperately to remove all thoughts of him from before—of what she'd lost. She sighed. "David, it was nice to see you. I really need to get my luggage."

She turned from him, head up, shoulders back, and strode toward the elevator, stepping in as the door closed. She leaned her head against the back wall and closed her eyes.

How was it possible that after ten years he could stir such feelings in her? Sophia took inventory of what she was feeling. There was a surge of attraction between them. Then the anger she'd felt for years accompanied the thought of him. She'd walked out on him. His betrayal was much stronger than the attraction. It had given her purpose to make something of herself. Her success as a concert cellist sprang as much from her desire to succeed as it did from a need to escape her feelings for David.

Sophia opened her eyes when she heard the elevator doors open. The small group of others who had been aboard the plane with her stood watching the empty luggage carousel go around. Sophia waited for her cello case to arrive in the oversized luggage. It killed her to have to check the instrument, but there were no other choices. It was times like this she wondered why she didn't play the violin. She could carry that onto the plane.

Relief flooded her as a man brought her the case. She quickly opened it and examined the instrument to assure herself it had arrived in one piece.

Her trip was to last two weeks. She'd wanted to pack only one bag, but against her better judgment, she'd packed two. When the two suitcases dropped to the carousel, she pulled them off and stacked them. One hung from the other, and she slung her carry-on over her shoulder. With a grunt, she hoisted her cello to her side. She started toward the curb to collect a cab.

Footsteps clattered on the tile floor behind her.

"Sophia."

She wouldn't let herself turn to see him hurrying to her.

"Let me help you."

"I travel like this all the time. I do not need your assistance." Her voice was cold.

"I wouldn't be a gentleman if I didn't offer to help a lady in need."

"A gentleman?" He'd already taken her suitcases from her and wheeled them out to the sidewalk. "Mr. Kendal, I assure you I do not need you."

"No, you made that perfectly clear when you disappeared and left your engagement ring in the sink." He kept walking, forcing her to follow.

"Where are you going?" She tried to keep up with him, but his long stride kept him a hefty distance ahead of her.

He pointed off into the parking garage. "My car is parked just over here."

"Your car?" She trotted to catch up with him. "I'm taking a cab."

"I don't want you in a cab in the middle of the night," he said, unwavering from his path.

She grunted and quickened her step again.

"I don't care what you think—"

"I know." He darted a stare in her direction.

"You don't even know where I'm going." She finally closed the distance between them and walked side-by-side with the man who had captured her heart for years. She despised him for it.

"Miss Katie's."

He pushed the button on his key and the lights on the Toyota Camry lit up. "Your cello should fit in the backseat," he said as he hoisted her luggage into the trunk with his own.

Sophia shook her head and opened the back door. She gently laid her cello case across the seat. David shut the trunk and slid past her to open her door. Her breath hitched as the air stirred from his presence.

"Thank you." The words left her mouth without the softness the sentiment should have had.

She dropped into the seat. He winked and shut her door before walking around to the other side of the car.

"Did you know I was going to be on that flight?" She wondered if she was a victim to a vicious plot to make her face him.

"No." The dip in his voice made her understand that he, too, was disappointed in whatever was going on.

"But you've talked to my grandmother enough to know I'd be here?"

"You forget who her roommate is." He smiled as he drove from the parking garage. "Those two women never stop talking."

"So, how is your Aunt Millie?" She adjusted the scarf at her neck as she peered out the window, awaiting his answer.

"She's fine. She's very happy to be with your grandmother again. You'd think by the way those two carry on that they were little girls and not the eighty-four-year-olds that they are."

"Eighty-three. They won't be eighty-four until next week."

"And that's why you're here." He started up the ramp to the highway.

"Of course. She wants a birthday party. I'm going to make sure she has the best one."

He laughed as she leveled her glance at him.

"What's so funny?"

"Those two will never change. You do realize they've been planning this party for a year. It's all planned out, but I think you are *their* guest of honor."

She shook her head. He had no idea what he was talking about. She'd settle into her grandmother's house, and in the morning, they'd have a long talk. If having David at the airport was another attempt at their matchmaking, Sophia wasn't interested.

"So, you still live in Kansas City?" she asked, watching familiar landmarks pass in the darkness.

"This is home." He turned off the highway and headed down the streets toward her grandmother's house. "What about you? Where do you call home now?"

She didn't like his questioning or maybe it was his tone. Then again, maybe it was because she didn't have an answer for him.

"My apartment is in Seattle."

It wasn't until they headed down the very street where her grandmother lived that Sophia asked, "How is your daughter?"

The words themselves hurt.

"She's wonderful, thank you. She just turned seventeen."

"I'm sure your hands are full with her now." The comment sounded snide, though she hadn't meant it to be.

"She's a good kid. She gets straight A's, she's employee of the month, and a volunteer at the nursing home. She was just elected to the student council, too."

"She makes you very proud." There was a stabbing in her chest and a quiver in her lip. Jealousy was ugly when it reared its head, and she hadn't known she'd still feel it so strongly. Her eyes misted, but she kept them diverted out the window and batted the tears back.

"I'm very proud of her," he said. "You know that her mother left us…left her with me, that is." He slowed the car in front of her grandmother's home. "That was hard on her."

"I'm sure it was."

"Sophia, you can't blame Carissa for what happened to us, if that indeed is what you've done." He pulled the car into the driveway and put it into park.

"I don't." She finally turned toward him and looked him in the eye. "I blame you. I completely blame you. Thank you for the ride." She put her hand on the door to open it, and he caught her other hand in his.

"Sophia, why did you leave?" By his grip on her hand,

she knew he'd waited ten years to hear her explanation.

The emotions of the day she'd left flooded back at her, slapping her in the face and squeezing her heart. She hadn't expected to see him today. She hadn't had time to think things out.

She extracted her hand from his and opened the door. She pulled the cello from the backseat as he lifted her suitcases from the trunk and then guided her toward the back porch.

"Why are you going this way?" she whispered, knowing the occupants of the house were asleep.

"Miss Katie doesn't like us to use the front door at night." He took his keys from his pocket and unlocked the door.

"Why do you have a key?" Her voice rose in volume and pitch.

He didn't answer, but pushed open the door and flipped on the light for the enclosed back porch.

David walked in further, turning on the light in the kitchen just through the next door.

It smelled like home. Sophia closed her eyes and soaked it in.

The house had been a boarding house when her grandmother had lived there as a small girl. It had remained one until Sophia was thirteen and her grandfather had died. It was then her grandmother had decided it was no longer safe to live under the same roof with strangers when there was no man to protect them. The decision hadn't disappointed Sophia in the least, though she'd met many wonderful people over the years including a cellist who'd inspired her life's work.

"Are you coming in?" David propped himself against the doorjamb as he watched her.

His lean frame, which stood just shy of six feet, hadn't

changed from her memory of him. The face she had known so well had a few lines in places that made her think he'd gotten them from worry. Had he worried about her? No, she decided. He was a father. Fathers, as far as she could remember, had those kinds of lines. The kind of lines that said to the world that they loved someone so much they worried often.

He removed his tie and loosened the buttons on his uniform shirt. Again with a wink, he walked back into the kitchen as she followed with her cello still clutched in her hand.

"You should go now. I'll be just fine. Thank you again for the ride." She laid the instrument across the kitchen table and steadied her eyes on him.

"You always said you'd be fine." He reached into the cupboard for a glass and filled it with water at the sink.

"What does that mean?" Her hands rested on the back of a chair to steady them as she watched his casual actions in her grandmother's kitchen.

"When I asked you to marry me, you said you were fine with the way things were. I bought that. You said you were *fine* not being first seat." He kept his back to her, and she could read tension in the set of his shoulders. "You were *fine* being part of the Kansas City Symphony, and you didn't need to travel or tour with those who asked for you."

"I'm not who I was ten years ago." She crossed her arms over her chest and let her fingers fidget with the edge of her scarf.

"You sure as hell aren't." He put the glass in the sink and turned to face her.

Their eyes met. He took a step toward her. She could smell him again. His breath caressed her forehead.

He reached a hand to her cheek and brushed it with his thumb. Her breath hitched, and her heart rate quickened.

He took another step closer to her until there was no space between them.

Suddenly, she didn't have it in her to fight him.

Gently, ever so gently, he laid a kiss on her lips. Her body swayed toward him. He kept the kiss soft.

A violent storm pulsed through her. He deepened the kiss as he wrapped his arms around her waist and pulled her to him. She still fit. His body was warm against hers, and just like the way she'd felt at home the moment she walked through the back door, she felt at home in his arms.

He rested his forehead against hers. "I've missed you, Sophia Burkhalter."

Then he withdrew his arms from her, and taking a step back, he shoved his hands into his pockets.

"Miss Katie says she'll be making blueberry pancakes in the morning. She usually has breakfast on the table by seven-thirty. I wouldn't be late. I'm sure you know the special pancake breakfast is for you." He walked into the darkened living room.

"Where are you going?" Her heart still pounded in her chest, and her body swayed from his kiss.

David stepped back into the light. A sly smile raised a corner of his mouth, and one of his dark eyebrows arched. She could feel the color rise in her cheeks.

"Oh, that's right. You don't know, do you?" He tapped his hand on the jamb of the door. "I live here, too. I know you can find your room. It's also where you left it. Good night, Sophia. Sweet dreams."

It was already eight o'clock when the smell of pancakes stirred Sophia awake. She opened her eyes and saw the room of her childhood in the daylight. Warmth filled her, and a smile crossed her lips. She was home.

It had been so long since she'd called anywhere home.

She'd known only three in her lifetime. The one she shared for such a short time with her parents. The one she shared with her grandparents after her parents died. She sighed. Then there was the home she'd shared with David.

The thought had tears stinging her eyes and a lump forming in her throat that she forced down. With a deep breath, she cleared her conscience. She'd left. It had been her decision to leave and start a life away from them all. It would be that same life she would return to in fourteen days.

She dug through her suitcase and found her warm, pink robe. She slipped it over her gray pajama bottoms and white tank top. Giving herself a glance in the mirror, she dragged her fingers through her hair and decided there wasn't much she could do with it.

She stood in front of the mirror a moment longer and studied the scar on her neck that had plagued her since childhood. She ran her fingers over it. The hideous mark was there as a reminder of what it had taken to save her life.

Her lips pursed and tears still stung her eyes when she thought about the accident that had put her in the path of death and had taken her parents from her. With one more glance at herself, she tightened up the robe, pulling the lapels together until her throat was covered. Then she headed downstairs.

Chatter came from the kitchen, and Sophia stood on the bottom step and listened. She closed her eyes when she heard her grandmother's voice. Her heart beat faster with the anticipation of her grandmother's arms embracing her. Too many years had passed since she'd seen Katie. Sure, they spoke on the phone every week, but Sophia had been so angry with David and had left in such a storm of emotions that she'd never been back to Kansas City, even to see her grandmother. Guilt that she'd abandoned her to escape humiliation ripped at her. She promised herself to make their time together memorable.

Sophia took a deep breath and walked toward the back of the house to the kitchen. She stopped at the door and watched as her grandmother fussed over pancakes, and Millie stirred together more batter from her seat at the table. David was already up and seated with his aunt. A cup of coffee rested between the palms of his hands. He was dressed in a University of Missouri T-shirt, jeans, and tennis shoes. Obviously, the comfortable attire meant he didn't have to work. The thought had Sophia's heart racing again. He'd be nearby all day.

"Well, well, well. Look who the cat dragged in." Millie noticed Sophia in the doorway and smiled.

"Good morning, Ms. Millie." She walked to the table and kissed her on the cheek. Then she turned to her grandmother, who waited for her with damp eyes. "Good morning, Grandma." She wrapped her arms around the woman who had meant so much in her life. They clung to each other for a long time.

Katie Burkhalter held her granddaughter at arm's length and took in the sight of her. "Oh, my little Sophie, look at you. You're more beautiful than I remember." She smiled and pulled her close again. "I've missed you," she whispered.

"I've missed you, too." Her voice wobbled. David crossed the room to the coffeepot, and she hoped he was too busy to notice her emotional greeting with her grandmother.

"You look like you could use this." He was standing behind her. She turned, and he held out a cup of coffee to her.

"Thank you." She took the cup without looking up at him.

Millie smiled from beyond her bowl of blueberries and batter. Her soft, blue eyes shimmered with mischief.

"What a coincidence that you were both on the same plane."

"Who said we were?" David raised his eyebrows at his aunt as she exchanged a glance with Katie.

They were at it again. Sophia shook her head, and Katie looked too innocent.

"Oh, hush." Katie pushed Sophia toward the table and laid a plate of pancakes in front of her. "Eat, you're too skinny."

"Oh, Grandma, you're the only one who would think so." Sophia laughed as David slid into the seat next to her and looked her over.

"I think she's right." He watched her from over the top of his coffee mug. "I don't remember you looking so frail."

"Frail?" Her mouth was full of pancake, but her heart was full of fury. She washed down the bite with her coffee and took a breath to give David a piece of her mind. At the last second, she bit it back, not wanting to upset her grandmother or Millie.

"So, did you two have time to talk last night? Did you make up? Everything back to the way it was?" Millie asked with as much enthusiasm as she possessed in her tiny body.

"Aunt Millie, things between me and Sophie have been over for a very long time," David replied.

A surge of two very different emotions went through her. First, the fact that he'd admitted things were over between them, which they were, infuriated her. That should have been what she'd gotten to say to drive home the point even harder after they'd somehow managed to get them on the same flight.

Then a gentle calm took over when she realized he'd called her Sophie. She lifted her mug to her lips to hide the smile she had surfaced when he'd called her that. It was the name those who loved her called her. The memory of him calling her Sophie had spiked a jolt of happiness through her she didn't know still existed.

The fluttering of happiness lasted only a moment and faded quickly when Sophia watched the figure of a young woman walk into the kitchen. Her long, straight, dark hair hung past her shoulders and over her face. Her shoulders hunched as she shuffled her bunny-clad feet across the kitchen floor. She had on nothing more than her tank top and a pair of cut-off sweatpants.

Black fingernail polish, half chipped off, coated her nails, and at least twelve black rubber bracelets adorned her.

The girl shuffled to the coffeepot, poured herself a cup of coffee, and then shuffled back out and up the stairs without one word muttered to anyone in the room.

David raised his mug as if to salute his daughter with it. "And now you've met Carissa."

All the joy in Sophia's body drained. Resentment for the man whose face had haunted her since she'd walked out on him overtook her. She turned back to her coffee. It had gone cold.

She'd met Carissa before. Perhaps he'd forgotten. It had been mere days before she'd decided to walk out of his life.

In fact, Sophia had been the one who opened the door that day.

Standing before her was a little girl with matted braids and dirty clothes. Sophia was sure she was there to sell them something, but the child looked up at her and said, "I'm looking for David Kendal. I'm his daughter."

Tears stung Sophia's eyes when she thought of it. David had dropped to his knees in front of little girl when he'd seen her. She'd whispered in his ear, and he'd embraced her. Moments later, they were running out the door without Sophia to help the little girl's mother. There had been the one phone call from David asking her to come to the hospital, saying he couldn't leave. She'd gone, just as he'd asked her to do, even though her heart had been broken. She'd stood just beyond the room looking in. A woman lay in the bed, a doctor attended to her, and David sat with Carissa on his lap, her head on his shoulder. She'd taken one step toward the room when a nurse had stopped her and told her that no one could go in except the *husband* and the daughter. Sophia left two days later. She couldn't stand the deception.

The man she loved was a father and obviously, according to the nurse, someone else's husband. She'd decided at that moment she didn't need anyone like that in her life. She'd be *fine*. Just as David had said she was.

CHAPTER TWO

The room seemed too stuffy to eat or breathe in. Sophia took her coffee mug and walked toward the front door. She stopped for a moment to look at the many pictures her grandmother had cut from the newspaper and magazines. In each photo, there she was on the arm of the sexy Italian opera singer Pablo DiAngelo. Her heart skipped when she looked at them together. They were happy. Everything about being in Rome was happy.

Sophia stepped out onto the front porch and sat down in one of the wicker chairs. She felt lost in her own life, but worse, she felt lost in the only place she'd ever called home.

The street was still quiet. All she could hear was the music that had turned on upstairs and rattled the windows.

It was selfish, she knew, but she wondered how much the teenager listening to Metallica knew about her. How much had the girl's father shared with her about the woman he had once loved?

Sophia snorted. Why would he bother? She didn't even mean enough for him to tell her he had a child.

It didn't matter. She'd be gone soon enough. For the moment, she was home and she would help her grandmother and her best friend throw the best birthday party ever.

The screen door rattled.

"You've been home less than twelve hours and have already left the room in a huff. What's gotten into you?"

Sophia wasn't surprised her grandmother had followed her out to the porch.

Katie patted Sophia on the knee as she sat down in the chair next to her.

"Just overwhelmed with being here. That's all. It's really good to see you."

"You should have seen me sooner. I've gotten really old in the last ten years." Her grandmother wasn't one to hold punches, but Sophia couldn't fault her for rubbing that in.

"I'm sorry. I just wasn't ready to come back." She sipped her coffee and tried to hide behind the mug.

"Well, you saw the world, didn't ya?" Katie sat back in her chair.

"I sure did, but I never made it to the Vatican." For her and Pablo, that performance was as elusive as a brass ring. She took a deep breath. "But, for now, that's all over until Pablo decides on a new venue."

"What kind of man is this Pablo anyway? What kind of man wouldn't let his best cellist come home once in a while?" Katie asked.

Sophia felt the sting of guilt wash over her. She'd always told her grandmother it was Pablo's schedule that kept her from returning. In truth, she simply couldn't face David or the place they'd called home.

If it hadn't been for Pablo deciding to take three months off to make some decisions on his next career path, she'd have forgone the party her grandmother had wanted to have and sent her a card. She was quickly realizing that the grudge she carried against David consumed her.

"Grandma, you know he's sweet man. We've been blessed to have had so many dates offered to us," she said, and Katie nodded. "You do know I met the Queen?"

"You wrote and said as much." Katie sipped her coffee, obviously unimpressed by the news.

"Well," she began, waving her hand as though clearing the subject away, "what about this birthday party for you and Millie?"

"It is going to be wonderful." The smile returned to her

grandmother's face and, likewise, to her own. "You know, the only time Millie and I didn't celebrate our birthdays together was when she lived in Germany while her husband was in the service."

"I'm sure you wrote each other though."

"Damn straight. How many best friends can say they were in the nursery together? I used to gloat because I was three hours and forty-two minutes older than her. I can tell you that's no prize anymore. Eighty-four." She let out a sigh. "Who would have thought it would pass so fast?"

Sophia felt the tug of long ago times and people as her grandmother spoke of her life.

"Why do you do that?" Her grandmother nodded her head to draw attention to Sophia's hands.

"Why do I do what?" She realized she'd been fidgeting with the lapel of her robe.

"The scarves. The clothes. Your robe. Why do you feel you have to hide yourself? Why do you work so hard to hide your scars?"

With a trembling hand, Sophia reached her hand beneath the robe and felt for the most obvious scar. Instead, she felt the Saint Nicholas medal that hung around her neck. Her mother had given it to her, promising the patron saint of children would keep her safe. It had worked. The only time it had left her skin was while she was in the hospital after the accident that killed her parents but only injured her.

Saint Nicholas hid under the high collars of shirts and scarves, tied just so to hide her scar. No one knew he lay against her chest and kept her safe. No one knew—except Katie and David.

She adjusted her robe again. "I didn't realize I did it anymore."

Katie pushed up from her chair and walked to her

granddaughter. She took the lapel of her robe in her hands and laid it open. "It's part of you. An amazing part of you. Be proud." She kissed her cheek and walked back into the house.

Sophia raised her hand to her neck where the scar stood raised against her skin on her throat. There had been a trachea tube there for a month, and it had left its mark just as all the other surgeries and needles had, up and down her body.

"I always thought it was one of the most beautiful things about you."

David. Sophia pulled her robe together as he joined her, sitting in the chair Katie had just occupied.

"I agree with your grandmother. You shouldn't hide your scars." He took a sip of his coffee. "You never hid them from me before."

"I showed too much of myself to you physically *and* emotionally," she bit back angrily.

"That's what people do when they are in love."

"I'm not in love with you."

"But you were." He leaned back in the chair and crossed his ankles. "Are you sure some of those feelings still don't exist?"

The air had become less appealing. She wished she were back in Italy with Pablo.

Keeping her robe pulled tight, Sophia stood. She let out a curse as she hurried past him into the house. "David Kendal, you have no idea of the feelings I have for you. The good Lord would send me to hell for them."

Sophia tried to make her way up the stairs without anyone seeing her. She needed time alone, and her hands longed for the comfort of caressing music from her cello.

She made it as far as the staircase before Millie called

her name. Hesitantly, she turned back toward the kitchen where Millie and her grandmother sat at the table.

"I guess you know we already started planning the party," Millie admitted.

"David said something about that." She gave her grandmother a pointed look.

"I knew you wouldn't come home unless I was making you plan." Katie smirked as she cut through her blueberry pancakes.

Sophia sat down next to the older women and set her coffee mug on the table. She was mindful not to adjust her robe.

"What's left to do?"

"We have the church's community room booked, and Carissa wrote out the invitations for us," Millie answered enthusiastically.

"So, you need food and music and decorations?" Sophia stood and walked to the drawer that had always contained pens and paper and pulled out one of each. "Should we do a buffet or a sit-down meal? We could cut costs if we prepare the meal ourselves, but then what's the fun in doing *all* the work? And what kind of cake do you want?"

Katie patted her hand.

"I knew you'd take care of everything. You'll do a great job. Now, David is at your disposal, and he'll drive you wherever you need to go."

Sophia's stomach clenched.

"But I could just drive your car." There certainly was no reason to involve David.

"Oh, darling, I sold that car four years ago." Katie began clearing the table.

"I didn't know." She felt lost again. "How do you get around?"

"David and Carissa. They've been a delight to have here." Katie patted her granddaughter's shoulders. "Why don't you head up and get ready. I'll tell David you'll be down shortly to go to the bakery to pick out our cake." Her grandmother had turned to leave before she could protest his participation.

"Millie." Sophia leaned in closer to Katie's best friend. "You knew he would be flying that plane, didn't you?" she demanded in a whisper.

When Millie dropped her head, wouldn't look up, and never answered, Sophia had her answer. She shook her head and kissed Millie on the top of her head. Once again, she was in the hands of the matchmaking duo, but this time she wasn't a willing participant.

Sophia hurried up the stairs for the second time that morning. Fourteen days. That's all she'd agreed to. In fourteen days, she'd be back in her small, dingy apartment overlooking the Space Needle in Seattle. Back to her corner of the world where she didn't have a physical reminder of why she'd walked away from David or the guilt that she'd never returned to her grandmother.

She showered in the bathroom attached to her bedroom. Her bedroom in her grandmother's house was almost as big as the neglectfully furnished apartment she dreaded returning to.

When she had managed to apply her makeup and tame her curls, she dressed in a soft cotton dress and slipped on a pair of sandals she'd purchased in Italy during her tour at Easter. After one last look in the mirror, she adjusted the necklace with her Saint Nicholas medal around her neck and reached for her light, silky scarf. She tied the scarf with precision that made her look sophisticated and hid her scars.

The moment she opened her door and stepped from her room, she ran headlong into the teenager she'd briefly seen that morning with earphones in her ears and an iPod in her hand.

Carissa threw back her head, tossing her hair from her face, and narrowed her eyes at Sophia.

"I'm so sorry." Sophia had her hand to her chest to calm the rapid beat of her heart.

The girl before her said nothing. Her double-layered tank tops and jeans, which had seen better days, radiated her youth. Her eyes were heavily lined and hid behind the long, straight hair that fell well past her shoulders.

Sophia straightened. "Carissa, right? I'm Sophia. Sophia Burkhalter. My grandmother is Katie." She smiled, but the sneer on Carissa's face made it difficult. "It's nice to meet you," she continued, but Carissa walked past her, down the stairs, and out the front door.

The silence made her feel as though she didn't belong.

She found David in the hallway fixing a piece of molding that, much like Carissa's jeans, had seen better days. She watched as he put the piece of wood against the wall and tapped it into place with a finishing nail and hammer. She'd forgotten how handy he was.

They had bought a house on Cherry Street two years before she left. It needed major repairs, and they put two years of blood, sweat, and tears into it. Together they had picked out paint, flooring, window covers, and lighting fixtures. It was going to be the home they would share forever.

Then she found out what he'd been hiding from her.

She signed the house over to him and walked away from the life they had built. For ten years, she'd been unable to forgive him. She still didn't know if she could.

"You look nice," he said, lifting his head once the

molding was secure.

"Thank you." Daring herself, she took a step closer to him as he stood and wiped his hands his jeans. "I've been instructed that you'll be driving me around today."

"What a coincidence. That's what I was told, too."

"I can just give you a list…"

"No." He set the hammer on the table in the hallway. "You're here, and we're going to give them one hell of a party. Let me wash my hands, and we'll get going."

Sophia nodded and went to tell her grandmother she was leaving.

When she entered the kitchen, Millie and Katie scuttled back from the doorway.

Sophia opened the cupboard, took down a glass, and filled it at the sink. She purposely looked out the window to divert her attention from her scheming grandmother and her friend.

Their planning and matchmaking had once filled Sophia's life with joy. She'd fallen in love with David Kendal then, and that's what the two women wanted now. But there were too many obstacles. She had a life and a career far away from Kansas City, and David had his daughter.

Carissa sat on the front steps, her iPod still in her hand and her head bobbing to the music that played in her ears. Sophia hurried to the car before the teenager noticed them, but just as she shut her door, Carissa's head shot up.

"Hey, did you still want a ride?" David yelled from his side of the car.

Carissa pulled the earphones from her ears and glared at her father, much as she had at Sophia earlier. "I want to meet Emily at the mall."

"C'mon, I'll give you a ride."

She didn't move.

Sophia rested her hands in her lap and bit her lip.

"Can I sit up front?" Carissa slowly walked across the grass.

"Sophie is already sitting there," he pointed out. "Lots of room in the back. How will you get home from the mall?"

The teen yanked open the rear door on David's side of the car and flopped into the backseat.

"Do you care?"

Sophia noticed him watching her in the mirror as he backed out of the driveway. She wanted desperately to ask him about Carissa, but she kept her hands in her lap, her eyes forward, and her mouth shut.

When David stopped the car at the curb in front of the mall, Carissa was quick to jump out, but so did he. He closed the door.

"I am not pleased with your behavior," he scolded in a hushed tone, but Sophia heard him.

"Why is she here?"

"She's Katie's granddaughter. You will treat her with the same respect you show to Miss Katie."

"I don't like her."

"You don't know her."

"I don't care." Carissa turned up the volume on her iPod.

He tugged at her earphones. Her eyes widened as they dropped to the ground.

"I will not have it, Carissa. I will not have you treat Sophia like this. You straighten up, or things are going to get tough."

She replaced the earphones without another word.

He opened his car door. "I'll pick you up in three hours."

"Fine."

He sat back down behind the wheel as they watched his daughter trudge through the doors of the mall. He puffed out a breath and raked his fingers through his hair.

"Well, that couldn't have been more awkward." He pulled away from the curb, gripping the steering wheel like he wanted to strangle it.

Sophia bit her lip. "I really didn't mean to cause any problems. Why don't you go by the rental car place, and I'll get a car. This is ridiculous."

"Forget it. She's bound to throw more than one temper tantrum in the two weeks you're here. She's a teenager. She'll be fine. She's really a good kid."

The words didn't fit the girl she'd met, but then again, she seemed to have a personal vendetta against Sophia, and who would blame her?

"Why are you living at my grandmother's house?"

"We're having a house built. It was your grandmother's idea for us to stay there while it was being built. It's helped us out a lot."

"A house for the two of you?" The question sounded dumb. Why not for the two of them? Heat prickled up her neck.

"Yep. It was fun picking everything out together. It reminded me of our house."

An ache erupted in her chest, and she had to look out the side window.

"When did you sell it?" Her voice carried a raw edge.

"As soon as you signed over your half of it." He slid his glance toward her. "You didn't know?"

She shook her head.

David guided the car through an intersection.

"It was *ours*. I felt lonely there without you."

"I assumed you would stay there with your daughter

and her mother." The words, hidden in her soul for so many years, were free, and they were bitter.

"I think you assumed a lot of things." She could hear the anger surface in his tone.

"You have no idea—"

"You made sure of it." He pulled into the parking lot and shut off the engine, but he didn't move and neither did she. "I have no idea what was going through your head. All I knew is my daughter needed me. And I needed you, and you were gone. I never thought you were a selfish person, but I tell you what, my mind changed when I came home, your closet was empty, and your ring was *in* the sink." He scrubbed his hands over his face and let out a breath before opening his door and stepping out.

Sophia followed him. She didn't want to fight with him.

She wanted to have a nice party for her grandmother and Millie, and that's what she was going to do. She'd let that keep her focused, and she'd try to forget about the pain David Kendal had caused her—and the pain she had obviously caused him.

David opened the door to the bakery, and Sophia slid by, murmuring a thank-you. She stopped abruptly. Surrounded by wedding cakes of every shape, size, and color, she tightened her hands into fists. Why should it matter that she was with the man she'd once vowed to love and marry—and be surrounded by wedding cakes? It meant nothing. But the thumping of her heart told her otherwise. Their appointment with the owner of the bakery should have been for their wedding and *not* for her grandmother's birthday.

Two difficult hours later, they emerged from the bakery, having tasted every flavor offered and chosen three perfect cakes for Katie and Millie. Sophia had been surprised when David told her they had invited two hundred people.

"Carissa addressed all the invitations herself," he reminded her as they climbed into the car.

The same petulant teen she'd met this morning? "That was nice."

"She loves Millie, and she adores Katie."

"They're wonderful women."

David sat for a moment before putting the key in the ignition.

"Why don't we get some lunch?"

"Are you kidding me?" She choked out a laugh. "You can't be hungry. We ate cake for two hours."

"I could do with some real food. And from the look of you, you could too."

"What's that supposed to mean?" The smile disappeared from her face as anger balled in her stomach.

"You've changed a lot. That's all. You look run-down."

"Thanks so much." She dropped her clenched hands into her lap.

"Sophie, I just mean…ah hell, I don't know, but I think you need rest. I think the next two weeks will be good for you."

She didn't say anything else as he pulled out of the parking lot. After all, wasn't that what Pablo had told her when he had encouraged her to go home to be with her family? But would he have told her that if he'd known she'd be spending her days and nights with David?

CHAPTER THREE

Sophia sat in a restaurant, across from the man she was once to marry, and wondered how things might have been different between them. Had she not left, she'd never have moved to Seattle, and she'd never have toured with Pablo DiAngelo. That had been the highlight of her life—or so she'd thought. However, as she drifted into her mid-thirties, she wondered what she'd lost that day she packed her things and drove out of Kansas City forever. Beyond the pain of losing David, guilt still plagued her. She'd walked out on her grandmother as well. She'd intended to return, but the longer she stayed away, the longer she was in Rome, Paris, or London, the easier it was to let time pass.

She watched the riverboats move down the Missouri river. David had often held her close as the lights of the city disappeared before them. In fact, he'd proposed to her on one of those boats. After three years of urging from him, Millie, and her grandmother, she'd accepted.

She wondered if they would still have lived in their house. Would they live there alone? Would they have filled the house with children they'd adopted? Would the symphony have kept her happy, or would she have taught?

Sophia desperately wanted to ask about Carissa—and her mother. There was hardly anything she knew about it. All she knew was a small girl showed up and he followed, right out the door. So little had been said, but it was obvious by his reaction to the girl he'd known her. The thought still pained her. How could she ever think of marrying someone who would hide something as important as a child from her?

"Sophie."

She looked at him, realizing he'd been speaking.

"I was asking if you'd like some bread?"

She shook her head. "My head is still swimming from the sugar in the cakes."

"Now that was fun," he said, biting into the bread and raising a brow.

"I can't believe it took that long. I can't imagine if we were picking out a wedding cake..." She caught herself before more words tumbled from her mouth.

"Yeah, that would've taken even longer."

"I'm sorry." Warmth rose in her cheeks. "I didn't mean to..."

"Sophie, I got over it a long time ago."

The ringing of his cell phone was a welcome disturbance.

"Carissa? I'm having lunch with Sophie." His eyebrows knit together, and he shook his head.

"I'll come pick you up in twenty minutes. Will you be okay until then?" He waited for her reply. "I love you."

Sophia felt the knot in her throat as she heard him say the words to his daughter. *I love you.* The burning sting of jealousy ran through her and then the ache of humiliation. How could she be jealous? It was the man's daughter on the phone, not some lover that had replaced her.

She was the one who'd left and replaced him with a life and a career far away from him.

"I hope you don't mind. I need to pick up Carissa at the mall. It seems her *boyfriend* has just been caught making out in the back of the food court with her so-called *best* friend. She's a bit distraught." He motioned to the server to bring their check. "I can call a cab for you so that you can finish your meal."

Broken hearts happened to everyone, she realized.

There was no age or sex bias. At Carissa's age, she'd had friends to go to when her heart was broken, but Carissa's heartache had been caused by her friend. Neither she nor Carissa had had a mother to run to. Would that have made it easier to cope with? A part of her wished the girl didn't dislike her so much. Perhaps she could have been that shoulder to cry on.

"I'd rather go with you, if you don't mind."

He laid the money on the table and pushed back to help her with her chair. "I warn you, a seventeen-year-old with a broken heart isn't pretty."

"I'm sure she'll be fine. We all recover."

"Some of you do." He was four steps ahead of her when he said it, but the words socked her right in the gut. She'd broken his heart, and he'd never recovered—and he thought she had.

Carissa sat alone outside the entrance of the mall. Sophia's heart flipped in her chest when David ran from the car and scooped his daughter in his arms. Carissa curled into her father's chest as he walked her back to the car.

Quietly, Sophia moved to the backseat and watched as David opened the door for Carissa. He gave Sophia a glance that said *thank you*, and she returned the gesture with a smile.

Carissa sobbed, screamed, and called the boy she'd caught in the lip lock with her best friend every name that didn't include curses. Her restraint spoke volumes about her respect for David. Another pang squeezed Sophia's chest.

A few blocks from home, Carissa finally turned to glare at Sophia. Her eye makeup had smeared, and her nose and cheeks were red.

"Why is she still here? Didn't you get the cake?"

"We were having lunch when you called." David's voice was steady, but Sophia had to clamp her jaw shut.

"I don't know why those two old ladies think you guys have to do all the planning together. They'd be better off if just you and I did it." She crossed her arms and flopped against the seat. "She doesn't care." She jerked her head toward Sophia.

"I'm sorry. I don't care about what?" The cute little girl who had driven her out of David's life had turned into a miserable, obnoxious brat. And Sophia's heart ached for her.

"You don't care about the people you hurt." She turned and drove her unforgiving stare into Sophia.

"Carissa, that's enough." David angled his glance at his daughter.

"No, Dad, she asked."

"That's right," Sophia agreed, and then turned her attention back to Carissa. "And just who have I hurt?" The words tumbled out of her mouth, and she wished they hadn't.

"Oh, you're a genius, aren't you?" Carissa bounced against the seat again. "You knew Miss Katie thought you'd given up on her. She was sad for a lot of years."

"Carissa." He was warning her, but she continued.

"My mom said you were a—"

"I said that's enough!" David finished his daughter's bashing of her. "You will not talk to each other like this." The warning went both ways, making Sophia feel small.

He pulled into the driveway, and Carissa jumped from the car before David had put it in park. She slammed the door behind her and stomped toward the house, disappearing inside.

Sophia climbed from the car and slammed her door, too. David caught her by the arm.

"You're not seventeen. Don't act like this."

"I know your daughter is hurting. That doesn't mean she can attack me, and I have to take it."

"No, you don't." He tightened his grip. "But you have to know her vision of you is clouded. Give her time."

"By all means. I'm leaving in twelve days, and neither of you will have to worry about me." She broke free of his grip and stormed into the house, tears stinging her eyes.

In the privacy of her room, Sophia's head was spinning and her heart was pounding. If the rest of her stay at her grandmother's was going to be like today, she'd rather go back to her empty apartment in Seattle and prepare for Pablo's new venue. She closed her eyes and tried to steady her shaky breaths.

With Pablo in mind, she dug through her purse to find her phone. She dialed his number, but there was no answer. It was probably for the best. Her emotions were raw, and he'd pick up on that. The Italian curses would fly if he knew David and his daughter had upset her.

And she wasn't ready to probe into why Carissa's outburst had affected her so deeply. She opened her cello case and set up near the window. Straddling the instrument, she held the bow in her right hand and leaned into it.

The deep hum filled her ears as she pulled the bow across the strings. She closed her eyes and played through Pablo's last concert.

Every note was a memory on her fingertips, played with precision and warmth.

When she played, she was in a bubble. There was only her, her cello, and the music they created together. The world around her was blocked out for that time. Music hypnotized her and set her free.

An hour passed and crept into a second. Every muscle

in her body that had been tense was now liquid and soft. Even as she played the music that was so familiar to her, her mind wandered.

She thought of David and how they were before she left. They were one. They'd been in love, and love had been wonderful.

When he touched her, electricity sped through her veins. He was gentle and considerate, and he loved her as fully as she loved him. They were to wed and be partners in life—forever.

The beautiful image seemed so skewed. How could things have gone so badly? Why had David hidden his daughter from her?

His daughter.

What pain could Sophia have ever have caused Carissa to have the girl react to her in such a way? In fact, Sophia thought, Carissa should love her. After all, she walked away from the man she loved so he could be with his daughter…and her mother.

The notes Sophia played strained, and she tossed her head back as she finished what would be her solo on stage.

She'd been aware that when she'd left, the little girl and *her mother* moved into Sophia and David's home. They both should have thanked her for getting out of their way.

The last note was long and she drew it out, letting the stress in her body draw out with it. She had her music. She had her career. She had Pablo. They were all she needed.

She stored her bow and wiped down her instrument, her fingers aching. Her grandmother would be waiting dinner on her. No one would ever interrupt her playing, and guilt began to flood her senses as she realized she'd been playing all afternoon.

She fixed up her hair and wiped the makeup smudges from under her eyes before opening the door to her room.

David stood against the wall with his arms crossed over his chest and a beautiful smile on his lips.

She shut the door behind her. "What are you doing?"

"Listening." He moved from the wall, taking a step toward her that put them face-to-face. "God, you're amazing."

"I don't think…"

He cut off her words with a gaze that locked her eyes to his. Her heart slammed into her chest as she felt her lip quiver. Anticipation flooded her when she thought about him. She longed to kiss him again, and his eyes seemed to register the same thought.

David moved to her, their bodies now lightly touching. He reached for her, touched her face, and rested his other hand on her waist.

"You had a bigger audience."

"I did?" Her words were unsteady. His hands were on her. His body was so near she could feel the heat he gave off.

He nodded, stroking her hair, and then dropping his hand. "Carissa was listening until she left for work."

"Was the music bothering her?"

He laughed. "Quite the contrary. She plays cello."

"She does?" Her voice wavered, an aftershock of attraction jolting through her system.

"Don't expect her to admit it, but she plays because of you."

"I don't understand. She hates me."

"You've always been a big part of her life. We used to watch those PBS specials with Pablo DiAngelo so we could see you."

"You did?"

"I missed you." He slid his hand off her waist and grasped her fingers. "She knew the music was special to me, and once she was old enough, she asked me what instrument my friend on TV played. I told her the cello, and she signed up. It pissed her mother off." He smiled, but it was sad. "She's enamored by you, but she'll be horrible to you while you're here. She's a teenager, and now she's a teenager with a broken heart."

"The boyfriend?"

"Ex-boyfriend. I gather she stepped into the middle of that kiss and gave them both a piece of her mind before calling me." His pride showed, and it had Sophia stiffening to keep herself from sulking.

David stepped back and released her hand from his. He'd changed into a pair of khakis and a blue, button-down shirt that accentuated the breadth of his shoulders.

"You played past dinnertime. The ladies ate without you."

"I should have paid better attention to the time," she admitted, feeling the pang of guilt burn in her stomach. "It's a bad habit of mine."

"I remember. I'd like to take you out, if you'd consider going on a date with me."

"A date?" She shook her head.

"Dinner with an old friend?"

"I am a little hungry." What could it hurt, she wondered as she stood in the hallway looking at the man she'd thought of every day since she'd left. It was only dinner, though part of her wished it could be more. "I think that would be lovely."

He took her hand in his, and it felt natural. They walked down the stairs. They didn't say goodbye to anyone, just let themselves out the front door.

But it wasn't a secret. Loving eyes watched after them. The plans of two old women were moving in the right direction.

The maître d' of the restaurant that Sophia and David had once frequented led them to a secluded booth with soft lighting. David took her hand, and her pulse fluttered as he laced their fingers together for a moment before they slid into the seats on opposite sides of the table.

Sophia sank into the booth, aware of David's gaze settling on her. He smiled that sexy smile that made her insides flip.

The waiter arrived at the table with a bottle of wine, and David gave his approval. Sophia watched as he filled their glasses and then retreated.

"What's going on? Reservations? One of our favorite places? Bottle of wine brought right to the table?"

"Just taking a beautiful woman out to dinner." He lifted his glass and clinked it against hers before taking a sip.

"You planned all this out."

"The minute you and Carissa stopped fighting when we got home."

"Why?"

"Because I've missed you, and I wanted time alone with you." He reached across the table and took her hand again. "I wanted to ask you why you destroyed my life and walked out on me."

Sophia threw her napkin on the table and lurched out of the booth, but David was quicker. He scooted around the table and hemmed her in with his body.

"I'm sorry. I'd practiced that to come out differently." He took a deep breath. "You walked out of my life and stayed away for ten years, without a word. The least you can do is sit with me, have dinner, and answer a few questions."

Her jaw tightened, and she crossed her arms and rested them on the table. David took his seat once more.

The waiter arrived to take their order. David ordered

for both of them and then drank down his glass of wine.

"I'm sorry. You're not ready to talk about it. Let's just have a nice dinner, like we used to."

She bit the inside of her cheek. There was so much she wanted to say, and at the same time, nothing to say. His question was quite possibly as valid as hers were. She'd bide her time and try to remain calm.

"When did you change airlines?" She raised her glass to her lips, trying to ease the friction between them.

His eyes darkened in response to her retreat.

"Eight years ago. They had benefits, and I needed them for Carissa and Mandy."

Mandy. It was the first time she'd ever heard the name of Carissa's mother. Sophia swallowed the lump in her throat.

"That does make a difference." She sipped her wine again, wishing it to numb her quickly. "And my grandmother knew you'd be the pilot of that flight she booked me on?"

"Actually that was Millie. I had no idea..." He stopped when her lips curled into a smile.

"I know. I think they're still under the impression that their matchmaking skills are intact."

David nodded. "What about you? When did you become Pablo DiAngelo's cellist?"

Sophia was sure he already had his answer.

"He'd remembered me from when I played here with the symphony, and he came looking for me about the time I'd left."

"I knew he was trouble."

"What does that mean?"

"When he came through town and you played with him, I knew he was infatuated with you."

She shook her head. "I hardly think the few evenings he

was here were reason for you to fret."

"Sophie, you were starstruck. How could you see what was going on around you?" David poured more wine into his glass. "Do you remember when he took us to dinner? It was as though there were only two of you in the whole restaurant."

The waiter delivered their dinners, and Sophia immediately took her first bite. She was afraid if she didn't fill her mouth she'd say something horrible.

"You know, it's hard to find people when they disappear without a word."

"You looked for me?"

"I never stopped." His voice dropped to a whisper. "I thought you knew how I felt about you."

David cut into his dinner, and she could see his hands shaking.

"You didn't even tell Katie where you were."

The guilt she'd been fighting washed over her and threatened to pull her under.

"I didn't know you looked for me." Her eyes welled with tears, and she struggled to push them back.

Could he simply not see what had happened to them? Yes, she'd walked away, but the reasons were obvious. Otherwise she would have fought for him. He'd lied to her. He'd filled their relationship with deceit.

"You watched us on TV. You knew where I was." She figured she'd trapped him in a lie, but his eyes remained heated.

David wiped his mouth and set his napkin in his lap. "Only after some entertainment show did a special on the *superior voice of Pablo DiAngelo*. They showed pictures of you living with him in a chateau outside of Paris. He had his arm around your waist, and you were laughing." He jabbed his fork into his pasta, and then raised his eyes to meet hers again. "I'd seen that look in your eyes once, when we were happy like that."

"Do you think I left you for Pablo?" Now her voice had dropped to a whisper.

"Yes."

Heat ran through her veins. She couldn't breathe. She loosened the scarf at her neck enough to allow herself more air as she began shoving food around on her plate.

"You're not going to deny it?"

She looked up at him. His eyes held the disappointment that carried in his voice.

"I didn't leave to be with Pablo."

"But you're lovers." The accusation was there, and it was wrenching. She'd hurt him when she left. But she'd been hurting when she left.

She couldn't deny what he'd seen on television. She was happy with Pablo. She'd always been happy with Pablo, and once she had been convinced that Pablo loved her.

"I want you to take me home." She dropped her napkin on the table and walked out of the restaurant.

Carissa slammed the door of her co-worker's car. Would it have been too much for her father to pick her up from work? She should have been priority, not his old girlfriend.

The car pulled away, and she shuffled in the dim moonlight toward the porch. Dad's car wasn't back. If he was with Sophia, she was going to let them have it.

When he pulled into the driveway a few minutes later, Sophia fled from the car. Her dad hurried around the front of the car and caught her, wrapping her in his arms and pulling her to him.

She pushed against his chest. Tears ran down her face as she tried to run, but he held her tight against him. He'd never held on to her mom like that. Something nasty and mean burned in Carissa's stomach.

"Dammit, we are going to talk!" her father said in an animate tone.

"I don't have one thing to say to you." Sophia's voice broke.

"Then admit you left me for Pablo."

"I didn't."

"Tell me you didn't live with him, and that you aren't lovers."

"You are the biggest idiot I've ever known." She pushed him, and he stumbled before moving right back to be face-to-face with her. "I didn't leave that day to be with Pablo. I left because you lied to me."

Sophia unwound the scarf from around her neck and stood in the half dark. "You think the scars from that day are only here?" Carissa watched her point to her throat. "They're much deeper, and you knew it! You knew what I wanted more than anything in the world."

"You wanted a family. We both did."

"Right. I wanted a baby. I wanted my own baby, but that was something I had to give up. You understood that, and you respected that."

"I did. I do."

"Then why did *you* lie to me? Why did you keep the one thing I wanted away from me when you knew I would have loved her?"

Carissa's stomach knotted, and she pushed herself deeper into the shadows.

Her dad shook his head. "Sophia, what are you talking about?"

"You knew I'd decided I could still have happiness even if I didn't carry my own child. You knew I would be happy with the gift of a child, no matter whose she was."

"Right…"

"You had a child, and you didn't tell me about her. You were too ashamed of me to let her into my life. How could you?" She wiped at her cheeks.

Oh, God. Carissa wrapped her arms around herself. What had she done?

"I came to the hospital. The nurse told me I couldn't see you. I wasn't family. She kept telling me you couldn't take your daughter from your wife's side."

Her father shook his head. He raised his palms toward Sophia in supplication.

"Sophie." He moved in closer to her.

"Don't try to fix it now."

"I was never married to her." He reached for her.

"I know that now. Nevertheless, you lied to me. You hid your daughter from me. *You* left me for her when you ran with her in your arms and rushed to her mother, right from *our* front door."

Sophia's shoulders shook. "You always told me you'd never loved anyone like you loved me, but that was a lie, wasn't it? You loved that woman enough to have a child with her."

Sophia started for the porch. Carissa shifted back into the shadows and cringed as the woman who might have loved her like a mother stopped and faced her father again.

"What was I supposed to do? I wasn't even important enough to you to tell me you had a child. I would have loved her, David. I would have treated her like my own." Every word cut into Carissa's heart. "I loved you, and you lied to me. Pablo gave me an opportunity, and I took it. But it was after I'd left you."

She wadded the scarf in her hands.

"I loved you, David. I loved you so much. What you did to me hurt, and you can never take that back." She ran from him and into the house, passing Carissa without noticing her.

Her father stood still, as though he was unable to move, paralyzed by Sophia's words. Carissa walked toward him. Her heart pounded in her chest.

"Why didn't you tell her the truth?"

"It won't help. She believes I lied. She thinks I kept you from her." He touched her hair. "I love you. I want you to know I have always loved you from the moment I found out about you."

"But Dad…"

"That's it. I have to go in and pack. I have a flight tomorrow." He wrapped his arm around her shoulders, then let go, and walked into the house.

CHAPTER FOUR

Sophia threw down her scarf and pulled off her dress. How could he have the nerve to think she had left him for another man?

For a while she was Pablo's woman, but she was never his lover. She was too consumed with running from David, and Pablo was running from himself.

Sure, they had shared a few kisses over the years, but they were kisses brought on by joyous events, not by passion. She'd slept in his arms, sure, but they were usually on an airplane or train. Dammit, she wasn't the only one photographed with him. There was violinist Sandra Valdez and flutist Pierre VanVolden. Pianist Thomas Samuel was always standing next to her as well. But David noticed only the information that circled around her and Pablo.

She tore off her jewelry, scrubbed off her makeup, and started the shower. She'd locked her door, hoping he wouldn't disturb her for the rest of the evening—or for the rest of her trip, for that matter.

She was surprised he'd missed her at all. After all, once she was gone, he had a daughter and another woman to take care of. Anger washed over her, followed by confusion. She'd learned from her grandmother that David hadn't been married to that woman. She must have been important to him though. She was important enough for him to have a child with.

Sophia stepped into the shower. She let the hot water wash away her anger. She ran her hands over her skin and looked down at her marred body. She'd kept in shape by running in every city, state, and country she'd been in throughout the years. If there was a gym in the hotel she was at, she'd use it, but always in clothes carefully chosen to hide all her secrets.

Scars disfigured her thighs. Another scar ran down her side from her armpit to her hip. The one that had stolen the most from her ran from side to side across her stomach.

Sophia bit back tears that were in her throat. David had been the only man to see all of her scars. He'd run his fingers over all of them and kissed them millions of times. She was flawless in his eyes—back then, anyway.

She'd always understood that her injuries had made her barren. She'd never know the joys of pregnancy. She slid her hand over her stomach and wept. What would it be like to have the child of the man you loved? What joy did it bring to feel life grow inside of you? That bond between a child and a parent, what was it like on the other side of that equation?

If not for David's deception, she might have been blessed with him and Carissa as her family. But he'd taken even that away from her.

Four o'clock in the morning arrived quickly for David. He stood on the front porch and waited for his cab with his luggage at his feet. The sky was still dark, and the chilled air nipped at him through his uniform.

He looked up at Sophia's window and shook his head. He'd actually thought he could charm her back into his life. Instead, he'd accused her of leaving him for another man.

She wasn't that kind of woman, and he knew it. Nevertheless, he'd never had another explanation. Even Katie couldn't give him a better one because she didn't know why Sophia had left either. Now he knew the truth, and his stomach knotted when he thought of it. Why had they told her Mandy was his wife? Why had she left without asking for his side of the story?

He checked his watch. He didn't have enough time to run up the stairs, bust through her door, and make her understand that…

He let the thought go. When Sophia left, she had broadened her horizons. Would she have traveled to Paris and Rome otherwise? Would she have met the queen if she'd stayed as his wife? Would she really have been happy as the mother of *his* daughter?

He bowed his head. Mandy had brought Carissa into his life, but he hadn't cared when Mandy left them. Losing Sophia had destroyed him.

The cab stopped in front of the house, and David walked slowly to the waiting car. His work would take him away from home for four days. That would give Sophia and him either time to cool down or time to grow angrier. Either way, she'd only have one week left in Kansas City when he returned. He'd decide while he was gone whether he wanted to pursue a relationship—friendship or otherwise—or let her walk out of his life again.

Carissa paced through the kitchen as the sun began to peek through the window. She'd started a pot of coffee and pulled out a pan for some eggs. She wasn't the least bit hungry, but her nerves were making her jumpy.

"What are you doing up? It's only six thirty." Millie shuffled into the kitchen. Carissa met her with a smile and a kiss on the cheek.

"I couldn't sleep." She poured her great-aunt a cup of coffee as Millie sat in her chair at the table.

"Are you taking over kitchen duty this morning?" Katie smiled at her as she, too, entered the kitchen. Carissa kissed her as well and poured her a cup of coffee as she sat down.

"Yes, I guess I am. How do you like your eggs?"

"Very runny with toast."

"So, what kept you up?" Millie asked.

Carissa wasn't sure how much to say, but she knew they would understand better than anyone would. Instead of making breakfast for the women, she poured herself a cup of coffee and sat down across from them.

"Dad and Sophia had an argument last night." She felt the muscles in her neck tense and the ache in her chest when she thought about the pain on her father's face and the anger in Sophia's.

"That would explain the slamming doors." Millie laughed.

"Well, it looks like maybe we've failed our mission," Katie said as she stirred sugar into her coffee.

Carissa lifted her chin and watched the women exchange glances.

"Mission?"

"Katie and I were trying to get those two back together," Millie admitted. "It worked once, and we thought maybe it would work again."

"But she hates my dad, and he can't forgive her for leaving." But what if they worked it out somehow? Carissa rubbed her mug between her hands like you'd rub a genie's lamp.

"Oh, I don't think she hates him. She's very guarded," Katie defended her granddaughter.

"Tell me about her. She said something to him about scars. I didn't see any, but what was she talking about?" Carissa inched over the table to focus in on Katie.

"When she was a little girl, she was in a car accident with her parents. They both died."

Carissa gasped. "That's terrible."

"Her father was my only child." Katie took a deep breath, and Millie laid her hand over Katie's.

Katie told her about the accident and the injuries that

Sophia sustained that day. Carissa bit her lip to keep it from quivering. What if her own dreams of having a family were one day stripped from her as Sophia's had been? She'd be guarded, too.

"She wanted children of her own?"

"Yes, and your father did too. That's why she wouldn't marry him," Millie chimed in. "She didn't want him to give up his own chance of having children, but he loved her and that's all that mattered. As long as he could have her, he'd have everything he needed."

"But your father had never told her about you, and that was what hurt her."

"How could he tell her?" Carissa's eyes widened. "He didn't know I even existed." She twisted her fingers through her hair.

Carissa thought of the day she'd knocked on his door in desperation. She'd hated her mother for what she was and hated him, too, for deserting her. But when he saw her, he dropped to his knees and pulled her to him.

Her life changed in a moment. There was an instant bond, and she fell in love with him. She didn't want to love him, but she did.

"My mom said he'd left us. She said that maybe when I was all grown up I could find him."

"You did."

"Only because she was so strung out she almost killed us both. He saved us. He took care of both of us. He didn't have to do that, but he did."

"Because he loved you, and was so happy to have you in his life," Millie confirmed.

"But he lost Sophia over it. She left him because she thought he lied."

The women nodded, and Carissa sat back in her chair. She wiped her eyes. She loved her father. The feelings she had for him were so different from the ones she'd had for her mother.

Her mother was anything but a compassionate woman; one who never should have had children. Carissa didn't remember her life before David too well, but she remembered there were others around always. She remembered women with long, stringy hair and missing teeth cooing over her and taking care of her. Many "uncles" stayed wherever she was. They rushed her to bed so the adults could talk and have adult time without her. She'd only been seven when she'd knocked on David's door. Seven, she realized, was so young.

With a deep, cleansing breath, she looked at the women who'd taken her into their home and their lives. Her father deserved more than what he'd been given. He deserved happiness in his life with a woman—a woman he loved. With Sophia.

"Okay, I'm in. I'll help you set them up." Carissa stood up and dumped out her mug. "I haven't been very nice to her, so I don't know if I'll be much help. But let's make them fall in love. They both deserve this."

The older women laughed.

"Well, I guess we'd better make a plan," Katie said. "We have four days to make Sophia start missing your daddy and want to run into his arms when he returns."

Carissa kissed her cheek, ready to make it all happen—again.

By the time Sophia made it downstairs, only her grandmother remained in the kitchen.

"Well, you *are* still here. I thought maybe you'd left us." She smiled as Sophia kissed her soft cheek.

"I had a rough night." Sophia poured herself a cup of coffee and sat down next to her grandmother.

She'd dressed in a pink sundress and adorned her neck with enough strands of pearls that she would sink to the bottom of the ocean if pushed in.

"How was your dinner?"

"Awful. That man and I can't have a conversation without it ending in an argument. I just need to steer clear of him for the next week, and I'll be fine."

"Well, that should be easy enough. He's gone for the next four days," Katie offered.

"Four days?" Elation and disappointment filled Sophia. She wasn't sure which one was less appropriate.

"Yes. He swapped shifts around so he could be here for the party. He's going to have to turn most of the planning over to you though."

"Right." She was drowning in her own feelings. "Really, we only have the food left. We thought we'd go light."

"Sounds wonderful. Anything you chose will be perfect." She patted Sophia's hand. "He left his car for you. The keys are on the rack by the door."

"Great." She sipped her coffee.

"Can I make you something to eat?"

"No. I'm not very hungry."

Sophia walked to the sink and rinsed out her cup just as a familiar sound touched her ears. She turned around and listened more.

"Is that Carissa?" she asked. The closed doors of the study muffled the cello's hum.

"Yes. School starts in a few weeks, and she's been practicing hard. She really wants that first chair."

"Of course," Sophia said, as though it was what everyone wanted. She listened longer. "She's too soft. She needs to pull her bow longer." The notes fell into a familiar pattern. "That's one of Pablo's pieces."

"She's only just started that one. She's a little weak on

it, but she'll improve."

Sophia walked from the kitchen and stood just beyond the glass doors to the study. It had once been her music room as well.

She watched Carissa play the instrument she loved, and the sound filled her with longing for what might have been. She had real talent, Sophia thought. There was potential in the girl who seemed to despise her so much.

Sophia closed her eyes and listened to the piece. She knew it so well. Her eyes would squeeze tight if the note missed a bit, but for the most part, it was perfect.

Then the music stopped, and Sophia opened her eyes to see the young girl looking right at her.

Cautiously, Sophia opened the French doors. "You play so nicely. I just, well, I had to stop and listen." She rambled on, bracing herself against the string of curses that would surely be flung her way.

"I'm struggling with this piece. It's my audition piece for first chair."

"I thought it sounded wonderful." Her opinion was genuine.

"Really?"

"Yes, you're very talented." She slowly moved into the study. "Pablo doesn't like that piece very much. He wrote it after a lover left him, but it's so popular." Nerves rolled in her stomach, and she rested her hand there to ease them.

"It's a beautiful piece. I've heard him sing it a lot. I don't understand Italian, but music is universal."

"That it is." Sophia was next to Carissa now, and she noticed her heavily darkened eyes were not bitter as they had been the day before.

"Would you help me while you're here?"

"Help you with the piece?" Her voice lifted with the shock of the request.

"I'm sure you have other things to do." Carissa slumped. "I'd understand…"

"I'd love to." Anticipation took over any bad feelings. She wasn't certain what had prompted the abrupt change in Carissa's attitude, but she welcomed the second chance to bond with David's daughter. "I have to be at the caterer's at one. We could start now if you'd like."

"I'd love that." Carissa grinned. "Dad left the car for you so you could run your errands. I'd be happy to go with you if you'd like. I don't have to be to work until six."

"That would be nice."

"Let me go get my cello, and we can play together," Sophia offered.

Sophia returned only a few minutes later and set up her instrument next to Carissa. The girl's eyes were wide, and it was at that moment Sophia realized Carissa had been guarding herself against her. Perhaps she had finally realized that she wasn't a threat to her. They might not be friends once she returned to Seattle or Rome, but while she was here, perhaps they could be cordial.

"Let's start here." She touched the sheet of music. "This is the hardest part of the piece. It's a decrescendo so that the voice can crescendo. You have to play it right or the mix throws off the dynamics. Now, even though you aren't playing with a voice mix, it's appropriate. If your teacher knows the piece, he'll know you paid attention to detail."

Carissa nodded with understanding. She aligned her bow on the strings, duplicating Sophia's posture. They pulled the note at the same time.

Millie and Katie sat in the living room, where they had grown old together, and listened to the cello duet. Sophia had won over Carissa and vice versa. They needed each other. They were bonding over music.

The phone rang, and Millie picked it up before it could disturb their private concert.

"I just wanted to check in with Carissa," David said. "I'd promised I'd call her."

"I'll let her know you called."

"Where is she?"

"She's practicing her cello."

"Well, she can take a break for a moment," he said sternly.

"Oh no," Millie retorted. "She's playing with Sophie, and they've been at it for an hour already. This house is filled with beautiful music."

She could feel a joy in her voice that hadn't been present in years.

David harrumphed. "I won't be able to call back until tomorrow morning."

"Okay then, call back. I simply can't interrupt them. Oh, David, they're playing beautifully and laughing like old friends. You should see this. You should hear this!"

She held the phone toward the music for a few seconds.

David chuckled. "I can. I love you, Auntie. Please tell her I called, and I'll call her in the morning."

"Goodbye, David."

Millie hung up the phone and turned to Katie, who beamed like she was wearing high-voltage dentures. "This is going to work. I swear this time they'll make it to that altar."

"Millie, you are a hopeless romantic."

"Well, hell, what else do I have? My time on this earth is limited. I know that. Before I die, I want to see that man happy with the only woman he's ever loved. And that girl deserves a mother who would love her." She snorted. "Besides, you're more hopeless than I am."

Katie patted her friend's hand. "Well, we've done our part. Now let's see what the man upstairs decides to do."

"Sophia, that was wonderful. Thank you for playing with me. Old Brown-Britches will have to give me first seat if I play this well." Carissa wiped down her instrument, caressing the smooth wood that seemed to transform into a living, breathing thing when she played it.

"Brown-Britches? Do you mean to tell me Professor Braunstiches is still teaching music at the high school? He was well over a hundred years old when I went to school there, and that was a long time ago."

"Well, he's still there and a bitter, mean, old man."

"Well, I see things haven't changed."

Carissa watched her move with elegance and grace as she stored the instrument as carefully as a mother would secure her child into a carrier.

"I wasn't very nice to you," Carissa softly said, and Sophia stopped moving. "I'm very sorry for the way I treated you."

"Carissa, there are no apologies needed. You do not know me."

"There's no reason I should have acted like that to you either," she continued as Sophia stood to meet her at eye level. "My father has been miserable since you left."

"Now, I don't believe…"

"Well, you should. I was a little girl with dreams of finally meeting my father and making him and my mother fall in love. I wanted that storybook family." She stored her bow in the case. "I didn't know they never loved each other, and that it wasn't going to happen."

"Carissa, you don't have to share this with me."

"I want to," she countered quickly. "My father never stopped loving you. I hated you for it."

Carissa slid her cello into its case.

"I wanted a mother who would take me to Girl Scouts and ballet. I wanted a mother who would teach me to cook, and we could have tea parties and matching dresses. What I got was a cocaine addict who got knocked up by some airline pilot." As the words flew from her lips, Sophia gasped and then her eyes widened. "You left him for no reason."

"Oh, Carissa, I had my reasons."

"I know. I heard them." Sophia's eyes narrowed on her. "I heard you argue with Dad last night. I was on the porch," she admitted with a quiver in her voice.

"I see. And you think my reasons were wrong?"

"I know they were." Carissa carried the instrument case to the corner of the room and set it there before returning to the stand full of music. "My father didn't know about me."

"I find that hard to believe. I saw the way he looked at you."

"It's true. I don't know anything about their relationship, but I do know that they didn't love each other and that my mother only used him for drug money. She told him she had a baby and that I died at birth."

"Oh, Carissa." Sophia sat down in her chair again, clutching her cello case.

"I'd come to the house that day to find him. My mom crashed the car on our way there. We were only a mile away. I think she was so nervous. I'd found out who he was and where he was, and I made her take me to meet him. Actually, I had a few choice words for him." She laughed a nervous laugh.

Carissa sat in the chair across from Sophia. Her palms began to sweat, and she rubbed her hands on the knees of her jeans.

"She took too many pills. She passed out. He ran back with me, and by the time we got to her, the ambulance and police were there. He was blindsided. But he wrapped his arms around me and never let go."

Tears stung Carissa's eyes. "He loved me, and I could see that. He loved me from the moment you opened the door and found me standing on your front porch. He didn't know I existed, but he understood who I was."

Carissa stood and carried the music stand to the corner of the room where her cello stood. She looked out the window over the lawn where she'd seen the rawness of Sophia's pain. "They wouldn't let him take me home with him. They had no proof that I was his daughter, and my mother was unconscious. The police were going to take me away." She stopped there. Anything else would make Sophia only think less of her.

"When he finally returned home, you had gone. And I was glad." Carissa let out a sigh. "I didn't even know who you were, but you were in my way. You were in the way of my fairy-tale life. When Dad finally realized you were gone, and not just ignoring his calls, we were too much into his life for him to turn us away. Mom needed help, and he needed me. I was happy with that."

"I went to the hospital," Sophia said softly. "They called her his wife, and a kind of pain I'd never known shifted through me. Then I saw him with you on his lap. He was stroking your hair. I think you'd fallen asleep. He kissed you, and I decided I had to go."

Carissa sat on the edge of the large oak desk in the center of the room and looked at Sophia. She hurt for her. "He was miserable. He was mad at my mom for lying. He was mad at you for leaving. I could tell I brought him joy, and that was all I wanted," she admitted. "When you released the house to him, we found a house for us. Just him and me. We picked it out. Mom came with us, but really, it was our house. Mine and Dad's. She wasn't there much, and by the time I was ten, she left us."

"Ten? Your mother has been gone that long?" Sophia's eyes were damp, and she barely knew Carissa. Her mother had never cried for her.

She snorted and shook her head. "He wouldn't marry her. All he would give her was a home and money. He didn't want her. He wanted you."

Carissa stood and paced the room, walking by the piano in the corner and running her fingers along the polished wood.

"Mandy didn't love him, and she hated me. She wanted drugs, and he'd started to refuse to help her. She finally realized it would be better to dump us both, and she left. I haven't seen her since, and I don't care. I have my dad, and that's all I need."

"Carissa, I had no idea." Sophia looked like she might be zoning in for a hug, but Carissa wasn't ready.

"I know. I thought you should." She threw her hair over her shoulder. "We watched you on television all the time. I saw the admiration in his eyes when he'd watch you play. That's why I chose the cello. I wanted him to look at me like that."

"He does."

"I know that now. Give him another chance, Sophia. In all the years I've been with him, he's never been serious about anyone else. He never met a woman he didn't compare to you. He's been totally focused on me." *And you.* "This is my last year before I go to college. I don't want him to waste any more time on only me. I want him to be happy."

"Carissa, your father and I are two very different people."

"Who once loved each other enough to want to spend the rest of their lives together. You could have that again."

A smile crept over Sophia's lips. She stood and gathered Carissa's hands in her own. "You and those two old women make quite a team. But I can't promise anything."

CHAPTER FIVE

Sophia's head buzzed as she navigated the Kansas City streets. She hadn't anticipated bonding with Carissa. For her to come forward with apologies and pleas for Sophia to fall in love with her father again—it was too much. Sophia wasn't sure it was possible.

Who was she kidding? There hadn't been a day in ten years that she hadn't thought about the man. She'd Googled his name a half dozen times to see if anything came up. She'd had one hit—a write-up in the newspaper about how he'd helped a sick patient on a flight he was deadheading. Otherwise, he'd quietly been living his life and raising a daughter on his own after Mandy left. Sophia could feel tears stinging her eyes again. She'd done what she'd done, and she'd live with that the rest of her life. She'd done him a service, she decided. Yes, she'd gotten out of his way. He'd been free to raise his daughter without *her* selfish needs.

Of course, she'd done her own things, forged her own path. She'd made a name for herself. Who would she have been in Kansas City? A cellist in the symphony. Sophia Burkhalter was Pablo DiAngelo's cellist, and he was the world's most recognizable tenor voice. He sang to *her* music.

The first tear broke free and then another.

But she could have been Mrs. David Kendal. The girl beside her could have been her daughter. She could have molded and shaped her. She could have had others, adopted them with the man willing to do that with her. Instead, she had taken the coward's path and run.

Her throat felt like it was closing off. She turned into

the parking lot of the catering company and stopped the car with a jolt.

Carissa watched Sophia. She hadn't said a word on the drive. Maybe when Carissa confessed so much to her at the house, it had been too much.

She only wanted the best for her father. Even if she'd never admitted it to herself, she'd always known the best was Sophia.

There had been fights. She remembered them. Mandy thought David should marry her. He knocked her up, and he should do his part. He'd mutter, "I am," and walk away.

Carissa had never seen her father look at her mother the way he looked at Sophia. One glance at him and anyone would know David Kendal loved the woman who sat weeping beside her. Carissa knew it, and so did the women who had put them in each other's path before—and again now.

"Sophia, are you all right?" She rested a hand on Sophia's arm.

Sophia nodded. "I'm fine. I'm a little emotional, I guess." She wiped at her eyes and pulled at the pearls that constricted her neck.

"Why don't you take those off?" Seeing Sophia's apprehension, she turned her hand over and pulled up her long sleeve. She watched as Sophia's eyes widened at the scar that ran across her wrist.

"Long sleeves, bracelets, or a bandana, that's how I hide mine." She waited for the reaction. It was always the same.

"Carissa, you didn't..."

"Nope, but it was the first thing you thought." She ran her fingers over the raised scar on her wrist. "You thought I tried to slit my wrists. You couldn't imagine what would make me do something so horrible." She looked up at Sophia who, with sad eyes, only nodded. "My mother slit her wrists. She only made a big mess in the bathroom, but she got her point across. Dad took care of her. People think I'm her. I'm not." Her voice somehow stayed solid.

"What happened?"

"It was really silly, actually. I fell off my bike going down a steep hill. Don't ask me how, but my arm caught in the chain. It ripped the hell out of my hand. I didn't break it, but I don't know how I didn't." She smoothed her thumb over the scar. "If I had a loving mother and a family who attended church together and went on picnics, no one would think more than I'd got hurt riding my bike. But I'm the daughter of a coke addict."

"That's not all you are."

"But you didn't know that. You didn't know that until this morning when you took the time to get to know me."

"I'm so very glad I did. You are so much like your father. I see that now."

Sophia pulled down the visor and opened the mirror. She studied herself for a moment.

Slowly, with shaky hands, she unclasped the pearls at her neck. A medal of Saint Nicholas revealed itself as well as her scar.

Carissa smiled as Sophia lowered the pearls.

"It's not that bad."

"I've never been convinced."

"Warriors have scars. They're a sign of courage and bravery. I know they expected you to die in that crash. I know you had to fight for your life, and you were only a little girl. I know you gave up *a lot* just to be here today."

Carissa turned sideways in her seat to face Sophia.

"After your fight with Dad, I asked Millie and Katie about you. About what you'd been through. You would have married him right away if you could have had children of your own, wouldn't you?"

"Yes."

"I'm sorry for your losses."

"Thank you. I'm sorry they've affected you. I didn't know…"

"Sophia, he never forgot you or what the two of you had. He's so proud of you." Straightening her shirt, she smiled so she'd look braver than she felt. "We'd better go in. They're waiting for us."

Sophia nodded and then looked down at the collection of pearls in her hand. Carissa laid her hand over them.

"Be a warrior." She pushed up her long sleeves.

Sophia laughed as she dropped the pearls in her purse, and they clinked against each other and pooled on the bottom. "Warrior it is."

They agreed on chicken, a tossed salad, and an Italian bean salad as well as rolls and drinks for the party.

"Thank God they didn't offer fish. Millie would have insisted on that." Carissa shuddered.

Sophia laughed and pulled her keys from her purse as they walked toward the car.

"What about decorations?"

"We could go to the party store and pick up a few things. We don't want it to look like prom, but a few streamers and table decorations would be nice."

"What about a photographer?" She opened the car door and slid in behind the steering wheel.

"I don't think anyone thought about it."

"I went to a wedding once, and they had disposable cameras on the tables. The guests could take pictures of the things going on at the table."

"I like that." Carissa buckled her seatbelt as Sophia

began to back away from the parking space. "You know, Mr. Benton does most of the photographs for the school newspaper. His sister, Mary Alice, owns the juice bar I work at. We could ask her if she thinks he would be our photographer for the evening. He's on the guest list anyway."

"Mary Alice Benton is your boss?" Sophia's lips turned up in a smile.

"Well, she's Krantz now."

"Yes, yes she is. Gosh, I've known Robert and Mary Alice Benton since I was six years old. And I think I knew Jeremy Krantz from junior high school."

It was odd, Carissa thought, that the woman next to her was a stranger. But she'd grown up in the house where Carissa lived. Everyone in her life was in Carissa's. Even the friends she'd left behind were woven into the fabric of who Carissa was.

"Mr. Krantz helps out with the juice bar once in a while, but usually he's busy with the fire department. He's the captain."

"Really? I remember him being a scrawny little thing."

"He's not scrawny anymore. He's a professional, too. He was one of the people who responded when my mother overdosed."

"Overdosed?" Her voice rose in pitch, and Carissa knew it was just one more thing she hadn't known her father had to put up with.

"Yeah, right before she left us. I found her in bed. She wasn't moving, and her breathing was too slow. I called 911, and the fire department arrived first." The very thought of what her mother looked like in that bed made her skin go cold. "Jeremy Krantz was the first one through the door. I was ten and had just gotten home from school. Dad was out of town. It was a stunt for attention." She shook her head and let out a grunt. "She was always trying to get attention. Just like when she slit her wrist. I could do without any more drama like that."

"How often does your dad leave town?"

"He's usually gone a week and then home for two. Things have been a little crazy with his schedule this month. He's making sure he'll be in town for the party."

"So where is he now?" They pulled into the parking lot of the party store.

"Today he's in Hawaii, I think. He'll layover there and then fly back to L.A. tomorrow. From there, I'm not sure where he'll be. He should be in on Saturday around dinnertime."

"You keep close tabs on him, don't you?" Sophia pulled the keys from the ignition and slid them into her purse as she climbed out of the car.

"Yeah. He calls me from every stop usually. Millie said he called while you and I were playing. She wouldn't let him talk to me because we were having so much fun."

"We sure were."

They found confetti to sprinkle on the tables and balloons that said *Happy 84th Birthday*. They put a small, disposable helium tank and ribbons for the balloons in the cart.

"Maybe we got too many cameras," Carissa noted as she cleaned off the shelf.

"Two hundred people are a lot. We'll need them."

Carissa nodded in agreement as a mother and her daughter walked past them. They were shopping for decorations for the girl's seventh birthday party, as the little girl kept saying over and over to her mother. The sight tugged at her. She looked over at Sophia, who was counting the cameras in the cart. Had she stayed, would they have shopped for birthday decorations or party dresses? Would they have had mother-and-daughter time? Would she have really loved her like she'd told David she would?

The little girl directed her mother down the aisle of princess party supplies. She picked up a tiara and placed it on her head. Carissa reached for Sophia's arm and pointed out the little girl.

"They need tiaras."

"Millie and Katie? Why?"

"Every little girl needs a tiara—to be a princess for a day—even if she's eighty-four."

Sophia laughed with a nod, and they went about collecting exactly the right tiaras for each woman.

When the cart was loaded, Carissa looked at her watch. "Oh man, I have to be to work in forty-five minutes."

"I think we have everything we need. I'll head home and let you have the car." Sophia headed to the checkout stand.

"Why don't you just drop me off? I can have someone give me a ride home. I only work a few hours today. It won't be too late."

"If you're sure."

"Yeah. In fact, why don't you come in and see Mary Alice. She'd love to see you. People ask about you all the time."

"They do?" Sophia's voice shook as she laid the items for the party on the counter as the cashier began to total their purchase.

"You're a celebrity around here." Carissa fidgeted with a necklace on the display by the register. "You don't think of yourself like that, do you?"

"Goodness, no." She shook her head. "I'm a musician. That's all I'll ever be." She handed her credit card to the cashier and signed the receipt.

Carissa reached for a bag, and they started out of the

store.

"You're much more than just a musician. People here see someone who made something of herself. You're on TV, and you have your name on how many albums?"

"Twenty-seven."

"Wow. Does the man drag you into the studio every week?" Carissa slid into the car laughing.

"Let's say Pablo DiAngelo enjoys his own voice and feels that everyone else should too." She backed out of the parking space. "He records every major performance and each album sells out. He's amazing."

Carissa watched Sophia's eyes when she talked about the man. Her eyes lit up and danced. She loved him.

"Is he good to you?" Her voice wavered.

"Oh, yes. He's been a blessing in my life." Sophia started toward the juice bar, following Carissa's directions.

Carissa thought of the fight Sophia had with her father. She figured they'd forged quite a friendship in the few hours they'd spent together. Would it be too soon to ask the questions that were now plaguing her?

"Do you love Pablo?"

"I love him very much." Her answer was quick.

"Oh." Her voice dipped lower.

"Why do you ask?"

"I was just thinking about the fight you had with Dad."

"Did you hear everything?" She only nodded and watched Sophia straighten behind the wheel.

"Sophia, Dad loves you."

"Don't say that." She pulled into a parking space at the juice bar. "It's been a lot of years. People forget what they really felt. Your father loves *you,* and he wants the best for *you.*"

Carissa shook her head. The woman was in denial, and until Sophia forgave her father for helping her mother, she couldn't convince her that he loved her. He'd have to do that himself, but she sure could plant the seed.

"C'mon, you need a chocolate-and-banana smoothie." Carissa forced a smile, hoping to clear the air a bit.

"Peanut butter and granola?"

"What?" She shut the door and smiled.

"I like my chocolate-and banana-smoothies with peanut butter and granola, too. Do you have those?"

"Yes." She opened the door for Sophia. "I'll make it special for you."

As soon as Sophia walked through the door of the juice shop, she recognized the old arcade. The thought brought a rush of fond memories. The loud, metal games had been replaced by quaint, metal sundry tables and the fragrance of fruit.

Carissa disappeared behind the counter and into the back.

"Sophia?" She turned when she heard her name and smiled when she saw Mary Alice. "It's about time you came to see me."

Mary Alice flew toward her with her arms held out wide to scoop her up into a warm hug.

"Oh, how long has it been since I've seen you?" She held her at arm's length. "You look fabulous. Just fabulous!"

"So do you." Her heart did a little flip as she noticed the generous sprinkling of laugh lines on her friend's face. So much time had passed while she was away. She'd missed Mary Alice, and she hadn't realized just how much until she was standing before her.

"I saw you on TV not too far back. What was it? Some cable special..."

"*Pablo DiAngelo Live from Monte Carlo.*"

"That's it!" She clapped her hands. "He's amazing and so handsome. How do you keep your hands off him?" she whispered.

"Every job has its temptations." Sophia looked around the quaint shop with its modern decor. "This is a great place you have here."

"Amazing, huh?" She shepherded her toward the counter. "This is where I met Jeremy, remember? It seemed like the right place to open business."

Sophia nodded. She remembered it was the day Mary Alice and Jeremy said their young vows that she'd first laid eyes on David Kendal.

She hardly knew he was there.

It wasn't that she didn't notice David altogether. She'd seen him, smiled, and moved on. Her grandmother had said to her, "There's Millie's nephew. Isn't he handsome?" She'd nodded and caught him looking in her direction. He'd just graduated college and was headed to flight school. She was headed to college. The matchmaking duo of her grandmother and his aunt wouldn't try their hand at setting them up for another four years. Her life would have been so different if they hadn't met. Despite the heartache, she realized getting to know him again, and getting to know Carissa, made up for some of the pain of losing them.

Mary Alice arranged the small display of treats on the counter.

"So what brings you into my little store?"

"I brought Carissa to work."

"Carissa? Oh…oh!" Her eyes widened. "Are you and David back together?"

"Well…"

"Oh, this is wonderful!" She reached for Sophia and pulled her into another hug across the counter. "He's missed you."

"We're not together. I'm only home for my grandmother's birthday." Her voice was softer, and the smile faded from Mary Alice's face.

"Well, I'm glad you stopped in to see us."

"So am I."

Carissa arrived at the counter with Sophia's drink.

"A chocolate, banana, granola, and peanut butter smoothie." She handed it to Sophia.

"Thank you."

Sophia handed Mary Alice her money, but Mary Alice pushed her hand away. "Oh, no. This is on the house."

"Thank you."

Mary Alice walked back around the counter while Carissa helped another customer.

"You have to come for dinner while you're in town. Come by and see the house. Meet my family."

"I'd like that." She waited for Carissa's customer to move from the counter. "What time are you done tonight?"

"I get off at nine."

"Why don't I just pick you up?"

"You don't have to do that."

"I have nothing better to do. I think I'm going to go home and practice for an hour or so, then I'll come back to get you."

"Okay. Sure."

She took a sip. "Yep, this is how I like it."

"It's how my dad likes them, too." Carissa wiggled her eyebrows.

The cold of the drink slithered down her throat, but the thought of sharing this small bond with David warmed her far more than it should.

CHAPTER SIX

David wandered in and out of the shops that lined Maui's Front Street. The surf crashed in the background, and scooters buzzed up the streets. Tourists from every part of the world jostled him; he'd probably brought some of them to their destination. It was a wonderfully eclectic place.

He stopped with a crowd out front of a store that sold hand-blown glass. A man in the window blew a bubble of glass into a small ornament.

Sparkling showcases of miniature musical instruments inside the window drew him into the store.

Behind the man blowing the glass, music played.

"Turn it up! Turn it up!" The glassblower's voice carried through the store with his thick Italian accent. Before finishing the sale she was completing, the woman at the counter accommodated him.

David listened. It was opera. It was unmistakably the voice of Pablo DiAngelo. A chill ran down his spine. Yes, it was Pablo DiAngelo's voice, and the cello was Sophia.

The woman approached him.

"Can I help you, sir?"

David shifted, startled. "I'm sorry. I was listening to the music."

"Pablo DiAngelo." It was a simple statement. "Do you know who he is?"

"Yes. I've met him before. Had dinner with him actually."

The woman clasped her hands together. "You've met Pablo DiAngelo?"

"Yes." He wished he'd been that impressed himself.

"Carlo! Carlo!" She shouted until the glassblower looked up. "This man knows Pablo DiAngelo!" The sound of shattering glass cut through the store, but she was still smiling.

The glassblower jumped up from his seat in the window. The beautiful ornament he'd been working on lay at his feet in shards. He kicked the pieces to the side, turned off the fire, and removed his protective glasses.

"I'm so sorry. I didn't mean to make you drop…"

"Ah, nothing!" He held his hand out to David. "You've really met DiAngelo?" David could only nod. "He is my favorite. He's amazing! He's…" The man searched for English words to fulfill his sentence. "Angelic."

"How did you get to meet such a man?" the woman asked, smiling and pumping his hand.

"My fiancée"—the words were out before he could retract them—"is his cellist."

"His cellist?" The woman's brows knit together. "Sophia Burkhalter? You're engaged to Sophia Burkhalter?"

"Was. We're…" He considered for a moment. "Very good friends now."

She nodded.

"Pablo is very in love with her. You can see it in his eyes and hear it in his voice."

The woman couldn't have hurt him more if she'd stabbed him with one of the shards from the broken ornament. It was painfully clear to him that it wasn't just about him and Sophia mending their relationship. There was Pablo. And Carissa.

He felt the energy drain from his body and wished he hadn't walked so far from his hotel.

"You say you are close friends?" The man stood studying him.

"Yes. As a matter of fact, she's at my home in Kansas

City right now."

"Come. I want you to take to her a piece I made." The glassblower walked him to a section in the store that displayed the miniature instruments made from glass. He picked up one of the cellos and displayed it in his hand. "Please, you will take this to Sophia Burkhalter. Please tell her that I am Pablo DiAngelo's biggest fan, and therefore, I am hers too." He handed the fragile gift to David. The tiny loops of glass must have taken him many hours to create.

"Sir, I can't take this."

"It's not for you," he reminded him. "You give it to her."

"But…" The man's hand rose in front of him, stopping his excuse. "I'll see that she gets it."

"That pleases me. She'll wrap it for you." He handed the woman the figure and patted David on the back.

"Make sure you put your card in there. She'll want to send you a thank-you note. That's how she is."

"And I will frame it on my wall." He laughed. "Back to work. I must start that vase over," he said with a shrug.

David waited for the woman to finish wrapping up the package. "This will give him such joy."

"I know Sophia will appreciate his gift."

David left the store, sat at the nearest bench down the street, and held the box in his hand.

What had made him walk into that store? They knew her. She was someone to them. Someone more than an accompanist to a man with an angelic voice, as the man had pointed out.

Who was he to think she'd leave all that and love him? She may have claimed not to have left him for Pablo, but with the shopkeeper's words resonating in his ears, he knew she'd replaced him with Pablo.

David felt a tightening in his chest, and he raised his

palm to it to ease it.

He pulled his cell phone from his pocket and dialed the house.

"Hello." Sophia's voice pierced his heart.

"Sophie?"

"David." Her voice softened.

"How are you?"

"I'm fine. Where are you?"

Could her interest be genuine? Would it continue? Could she continue with another man if she knew how he felt? Then again, did he even know how he felt?

"I'm still in Hawaii. Sophie, I heard you were practicing with Carissa this morning."

"I was." The pitch of her voice rose joyfully.

"Thank you."

"Thank you? Why?"

"She admires you. I know that meant a lot to her. You don't have to do it again…"

"I've already promised her I would. She wants first chair, and I want her to have it."

"Well, thank you again." He touched the box in his lap and thought of her face when he would hand it to her. "So, she's already at work?"

"Yes. She's off at nine. I told her I'd pick her up."

"You two are hitting it off?" The sheer thought of it amazed him. Carissa had made it clear that she didn't like Sophia, and David was sure the feeling had become mutual. But there they were, spending time together voluntarily. It warmed his heart to think about them getting along.

"We're trying. We practiced our cellos together and then picked out chicken and salad."

"Chicken and salad?"

"She went with me to the caterer. Then we went shopping for decorations and bought the ladies tiaras."

David stood from the bench and walked down the street, with the box in one hand and the cell phone in his other.

"Tiaras?"

"Every eighty-four-year-old princess needs one."

"I agree. One hundred percent." She had such a sense of fun. Something he and Carissa had missed out on.

"We shared some things, and I took her to work."

"What did you share?" The pain in his chest had completely eased, soothed by her voice. "You don't have to tell."

"David, the scars on her arms…did she really hurt herself on her bike?"

David found another bench and sat down.

"She showed you *her* scars?" He realized they'd bonded over far more than the cello.

"Yes."

"Yes, she crashed on her bike. The school counselor knew her mother had tried to commit suicide by cutting her wrists and put her through a year of hell at school. She was convinced she was lying, and I was covering for her. But, indeed, she wrecked her bike." The tightening in his chest returned.

"Well, she taught me a lot today. We were warriors together." Her voice had changed again. It had lifted.

"How's that?"

"She pulled up her sleeves. I took off my pearls. We were warriors, David. You know, those who have battle scars and live to tell."

"Damn, I wish I'd been there for that." He could only imagine how beautiful Sophia was. Walking with her head held high and sans the trademark scarves and pearls that had returned.

"It was exhilarating."

"I'm proud of you. Both of you."

"Thank you. Where do you go next?"

He would give anything to fly straight home to her arms. If she'd have him.

"I fly to L.A. and then layover in Seattle before heading back to L.A."

"You'll be in Seattle overnight?"

"Yes. Why?"

"Oh, well, this is really going to sound silly."

"What?" He stood from the bench and walked toward the ocean. Toward Sophia.

"Well, I forgot all about my plants. It was silly of me to have bought them, really. I guess I was just trying to make the place homey. But if you're that close, would you go and water them and check on things? And you can stay at my place so you won't have to sleep in a hotel."

She laughed, and he pressed the phone closer to his ear.

"What's so funny?"

"Well, you'd be laughing too if you'd seen my apartment. You may change your mind and go to a hotel after all. I have no food there. Maybe a bag of Doritos. I only have a bed, and most of my life is still in boxes."

"It sounds like the Plaza. But how will I get in?"

"Oh, well, you know me."

"You don't really keep the key above the door, do you?" He shook his head just thinking about it.

"No, it's above the neighbor's door. No one would look there. Right?"

"I guess not." He imagined her sitting at home with the phone in her hand, and a smile came to his lips. "I'll call you when I get there."

"Great."

"Thanks, Sophie, for everything you're doing there. I miss you," he said as he hung up the phone. She hadn't said it back.

Sophia stood in the hallway with the phone in her hand, the line silent. She pushed the button to disconnect and sat on the stairs.

I miss you. Oh, God!

She covered her mouth with her hand and let her body calm from the wave shock that had flooded her. She'd been so surprised he'd said it that she hadn't even been able to respond.

David missed her. How could she deny it? She'd missed him for ten years, but there was so much to think about now.

What about Pablo? He hadn't called her since she'd left. He'd been more than supportive when she told him she was returning to Kansas City, but he'd promised to call with word of new venues and a tour. If he'd heard good news about playing at the Vatican, he'd have told her the instant he knew. That lead to the question of what was happening to the career that she'd worked so hard for.

What about her dead plants in her sad apartment in Seattle?

What about Carissa?

Sophia ran her fingers through her curls and then down her neck. They brushed against a ridge of scar tissue, and she reached for her collar. Then she pushed it aside. Warriors! Warriors!

Carissa deserved to be happy after everything that she'd been put through. But would Carissa be happy if Sophia stayed? Or would she be better off if she left, again?

Did she want to stay?

Her heart began to pound in her chest.

Dammit, she'd left for a reason. The man she loved and was going to marry had a child with another woman.

Nothing could ever dampen the betrayal of that.

Millie shuffled into the hallway. She stopped and rested both hands atop her cane.

"Is everything all right with David?"

"What?" Sophia snapped her head up. "Oh, yes, he's fine."

"Well, that's good. Everything all right with you?"

All Sophia could do was nod.

"Good. I was wondering if you'd like to go with me tomorrow to the beauty shop. I could use a ride, but I know they could get you in for a trim if you'd like."

Sophia touched her hair and wondered if Millie was hinting at her, but realized she was just being polite.

"I'll pass on the trim, but I'd love to take you." She stood and caught sight of her hands. "Do they have a manicurist?"

"Of course. I don't go to one of those old-people places where they've never heard of such things."

"Well, maybe I'll get a manicure. Pablo would shoot me if he saw my hands. I don't think I've had them taken care of since we finished our last concert."

"Wonderful." Millie moved by her. "It'll be a nice day out for the two of us. We could have lunch out."

"That would be nice."

She watched the woman she dearly loved walk toward her bedroom and shut the door.

Not only had she not kept up the presentation of her hands, but her rigorous schedule of practicing had slipped too. The few hours she'd worked on it in the few days she'd been in Kansas City simply hadn't been enough.

She was spending too much time trying to make sense of her feelings for David. He'd be back in a few days, and maybe they could work things out. She wasn't sure she could get past his lies to a place where she could trust him with her heart, but maybe they could at least be friends.

She looked at the clock that hung on the wall. She had only two hours before picking up Carissa. She'd better make the time count.

CHAPTER SEVEN

The Seattle weather was as depressing as always. David had never seen a day where the sun had shined, but he'd be the first to admit, he usually didn't spend more than two hours in the state of Washington before turning for home.

He'd taken a cab to the address Sophia texted him.

David blinked away raindrops and stared at the dilapidated building. The security door stood wide open. An old woman sat on the stoop in a lawn chair, an umbrella in one hand and a cigarette in another. He stepped in a puddle as he crossed the street, soaking his foot.

Saddened by the squalor, he didn't even open his umbrella, but began his journey up the front steps.

"Who are you looking for?" the old woman asked as though she were the inquisitor for the building.

"I'm a friend of Sophia's."

"You're no friend." The woman looked him over from head to toe.

"Would you mind if I pass?" He tried to step around her, but she darted her umbrella to block him off the stoop.

"If you're a friend of Sophia's, I suppose you know she's up there waiting for you?" The woman lifted her eyebrows in question.

"Because I know Sophia very well, I know she's home in Kansas City where she belongs. I'll be staying here tonight without her."

"Smart-ass. Why is she in Kansas City?"

"Her grandmother's birthday party." Water began to drip from his hair and onto his face.

"Okay, big shot. Who are you?"

"David Kendal."

Her eyes grew wide, and her mouth fell open.

"Is there a problem?"

"No. No problem. Is Sophia all right?" She laid a hand on David's arm.

"Of course. She's fine."

The woman nodded and removed her hand. "Okay. Three-oh-three." She made a V with her fingers and pointed them at him. "I'll be keeping an eye on you."

"I'm sure you will."

"Don't hurt her again." Her words stung him as he passed.

As he climbed the stairs, he pondered what the crazy woman on the stoop had said. Had Sophia mourned him just as he'd mourned her? Perhaps he should have searched harder for her. Really, how was it that she'd disappeared without a trace for so long and then surfaced among one of the richest, most talented men in the world? Disgust with himself punched into his gut. He'd been as foolish as she had been.

David reached the third floor and found her door. He stood there a moment. Green doors with peepholes lined the hallway—each one the same. He found 303 and turned around to see another matching door right behind him. He reached up and felt for the key. There it was, just as she said it would be. He slid it into the lock and pushed the door open into Sophia's world.

He stepped into the apartment and set his suitcase to his side, resting his hat atop it. For a brief moment he contemplated calling her. Certainly, he had the wrong apartment.

A picture frame on a table by the ratty couch caught his eye. It was the photo of Sophia and her parents that had been taken only weeks before their death. She'd had it in the home they'd shared.

His hand dropped to the afghan draped over the back of the couch. Katie had made it for her. Those were the only items he recognized. He felt his knees go weak, and he sat down. Her scent rose around him. He realized she'd come to the home they shared with only those few items. That was all Sophia Burkhalter was then. And now?

David stood and continued on his tour of the tiny apartment. He saw the kitchen from where he stood. A window overlooked the fire escape, and there was enough room for one person to turn around and cook a meal. There wasn't even a kitchen table.

The wall in the living room had boxes lined up against it. Just as she'd told him, she'd never unpacked. He walked toward the bedroom and smiled when he noticed it was the most put-together room.

The four-poster bed was dark cherry and matched the dresser that was crammed in beside it. Draped on the bed was a handmade quilt, again a memento that Katie had made her. Her television was on her dresser.

Walking to the window, he pushed back the curtains. The Space Needle met his stare. The rain had stopped, and the sun shone through. He turned to see a chair in the corner with a book on the arm. He picked up the book, *Memories of Love: A Book of Poems*. He opened it and began to thumb through the pages when he noticed something fall to the floor.

David knelt to pick up the fallen object. Again, he felt his knees go weak, and he sat down in the chair.

His eyes fixed on the item—a picture of him and Sophia in front of their house. He stood behind her, his arms wrapped around her tightly, his chin resting on her shoulder. They smiled, and she held the keys to the house. Millie had taken the picture, he remembered.

The phone rang, startling him. He stood to cross to it

and then stopped and let the machine answer it.

"You've reached Sophia. You know I'd love to chat. Leave me a message." Her voice filled the small area. He could feel her all around him, and he smiled until he heard the voice leaving the message.

"Dammit! Why can I not remember your cell phone number? Oh, it has to be in this mess. Sophia, Bella, you must come home. I'm lost without you." The unmistakable voice of Pablo DiAngelo stabbed at him like a knife in the heart. "I love you. I miss you. Please, if you get my messages, call me, Bella. I need you. Ciao."

David felt sick. He wasn't sure he could stay there. He barely realized the ringing in his ears was the sound of his cell phone. He reached in his pocket and pulled it out.

"Hello." The fatigue of the past few days made his voice flat.

"David?"

"Sophie." Her name softened his voice, and he sat back on the bed.

"Did you make it to my place?"

"I'm here now."

"Horrible, isn't it?" She laughed, but his only thought was *yes*.

"Not what I expected. How long have you lived here?"

"Ten years. My plants?"

David stood and walked out to the other room. He noticed three plants with wilted leaves. "I think I'm too late. Oh, there's a cactus by the window. It might be hanging on."

"I call that one Pablo. Prickly and dry and hard to beat down." She laughed a full-hearted laugh, but David was silent. "David, is something wrong?"

"Pablo left you a message a few minutes ago. He sounded"—he thought for a moment—"desperate."

"Is he all right? I've been trying to call him for days."

"He just wants you to call him." He tried to swallow the lump that stuck in his throat.

"You'll be back in a few days?"

"Yes. I fly to L.A. in the morning, then from there to Texas to Chicago, and end back up in Kansas City. This covering other shifts to get mine free is really crazy." He tried to lighten the mood, but was finding it hard to do.

"Well, Carissa and I are going to practice until our fingers bleed and then go to the mall and watch some chic flick that the ex-boyfriend wouldn't see with her."

"Sophie, I love that you're getting to know her." Even as he said the words, he felt the warmth of tears stinging his eyes.

"It's going to make it harder to leave."

"Maybe you should think of sticking around. It's obvious this isn't much of a home to you." He wasn't going to hold his tongue about that. He was on the verge of telling her how disappointed he was in her. She'd made a beautiful home for them, so why had she neglected herself like this?

"No, it's not much of a home. I spend most of my time in Italy or on tour. Wherever Pablo needs me is home."

David bit down on his lip to keep in any further comments he could imagine from spewing from his mouth.

"Why did you move to Seattle?"

"It was far away from you," she whispered.

"Sure was." His heart was breaking as he walked to the kitchen. "Thanks for letting me stay here." He opened a cupboard and laughed when he saw the bag of Doritos. "How old are these chips?"

Sophia snorted. "Don't even bother. You should go down the block to Mr. Chan's and get some carryout. Best Chinese ever."

Her voice was too brittle, as though she were crying.

"Then I'd have to pass the inquisitor at the stoop." He opened another cupboard to find one plate, one mug, and one bowl. He shook his head. She didn't deserve to isolate herself like this.

"You met Mrs. McKinley."

"Is that what that was?"

"Sorry. She's a bit nosey."

"I'd say."

"I should have warned you. She's harmless really."

"I hope so because, after a quick inspection, it looks like I'll be eating Mr. Chan's or starving."

"David, I...thanks for stopping in to check on things."

"Thanks for the offer for the bed and free television."

"My pleasure. Goodbye, David."

"Sophie," he called out to stop her from hanging up. "Give some thought to moving back. You can commute from Kansas City to Italy or L.A. when Pablo needs you just as well as you can from Seattle." He leaned against the counter and tried to force his stomach to settle. "Not for me, maybe not even for you, but for Katie and Millie. Think about it."

"I'll talk to Pablo," she said after a long silence.

"Good enough." David balled his fist and shoved it into his pocket.

He'd rather use his fist on Pablo.

Sophia stood outside the study and closed her cell phone. There was some comfort in knowing where David was, and that alone was reason to agonize over her mixed feelings. Did she only miss him, or was it deeper? Did she still love him?

Either way, she could never be the most important thing in his life again. There was Carissa.

And, for the first time, she wasn't jealous of Carissa. Carissa was a wonderful girl, and Sophia owed it to her to give her that consideration. David had done a wonderful job with her. He'd taken a scared little girl and given her stability and love, just as Sophia's grandparents had done for her after she lost her parents.

Again, her heart began to pound in her chest with the very thought of him. There was no reason David would ask her to move back to Kansas City if he didn't intend to feel out his own emotions. She had to know what her future held for her. She had to call Pablo.

"You look lost in thought," Carissa said. "Is everything all right?"

"Yes. I was just talking to your father." She felt the tug in her cheeks and realized she was grinning

"Are you two working things out between you?"

"Well, we're getting along just fine, if that's what you're asking."

Carissa shifted her weight and hooked her thumbs into the back pockets of her jeans.

"Well, what if I was asking if the two of you were back together?"

Sophia felt her stomach knot. "Which side do you support?"

Carissa walked closer to Sophia. Before Sophia knew what was going on, Carissa wrapped her arms around her neck and hugged her.

"Sophia, you make him happy. He loves you, and I think you're still in love with him. "

"What makes you think that?"

"I don't think you ever fell out of love with him." Carissa stepped back and moved to the stairs and sat down. She patted the step next to her. Sophia took the cue and sat by her. "I pushed you away. I know that. I meant to. I meant to do it again, but I fell in love with you, too." She laughed. "Well, you know what I mean."

"Carissa, you don't know me."

"Yes, I do." She reached for Sophia's hand and held it. "Before I found Dad, I knew what a bad person you were."

"Oh."

"That was according to Mandy," she said, considering. "You took the man she loved and stole him away. I know that's not true."

"I see."

"Then what my dad said was different. Yes, he was angry with you for a long time. And then he was sad and scared because he couldn't find you. And trust me, he tried." *That confirmed what he'd said about it being hard to find people when they disappear*, thought Sophia

Mandy continued, "Finally, he had to refocus. He had to take care of me. He had to put me in school, find me doctors and friends, and include me in his family. He had to take care of Mandy so I would be safe and happy. But he never forgot you. He kept in close touch with Katie, and they worried about you together. I'm sure once you called Katie, his mind eased a bit, but he's always missed you. That's why I hated you for so long. I wanted him to myself, and I got that when you and Mandy left."

"You don't call her Mom?"

"She doesn't deserve the title."

Sophia nodded and looked down at their clasped hands. It was comfortable. Carissa laid her head on Sophia's shoulder.

"A mother loves and respects her daughter. She confides in her, and they bond. Mandy never did that. She tossed me around from friend to friend. Whoever would take us in. She lied to me about my father. She told me once that he died. Then she said he left. When I was seven,

I found out who he was and where he lived. Then she couldn't stop me from finding him." She blew out a breath.

"But that image of the perfect family was still in my head, and I wanted that. I always thought Dad would marry someone, and I would get that. But he only ever loved you, so I only got him. I've always been happy with just him." Carissa sniffed back tears. "I love my father so much. I respect him for all he's done and given up to give me a perfect life. I want him to have a perfect life, too. I know that that perfect life includes you."

Carissa watched her hopefully. "How much longer will you be here?"

"Just until Sunday morning after the party."

"Will you, for my sake if nothing else, see if there's anything left between the two of you?"

"Carissa, I can't promise you anything." She batted away the tears that stung her eyes. She wasn't sure what her feelings for David were. Each emotion was pulling her in a different direction. His betrayal was pushing her back to Pablo. His sincerity was making her consider staying. His daughter was winning her over. What if, in the end, she was a disappointment to Carissa? That would forever affect any relationship she would have with David.

"I just want you to be open to it and know that I'm very okay with it. In fact, I want this more than anything." Carissa tugged Sophia's hand. "Let's go for a drive."

"I thought we were going to practice."

"It can wait. C'mon."

Though Sophia knew Carissa had been driving for at least a year, there was a knot in her belly when she thought about being her passenger. But then again, there was already a knot in her belly.

"Where are we going?"

Carissa pulled out of the driveway. "I just want to show you something."

Sophia watched as familiar landmarks passed by them, but her uneasiness flooded back when Carissa turned down Cherry Street and pulled up in front of the house she'd walked away from ten years earlier.

"Oh, my God," was all she could say as she stepped out of the car.

"It's for sale." Carissa walked around the car and stood next to her. They looked at the house that had once been home to both of them.

"I can't do this." Sophia opened the car door, desperate to climb back in.

"Warrior!" Carissa's word stopped her. "Don't run away again. I know it's in you to hide, but no more running."

Anger started to boil in her stomach, and the knot pulled tighter. How could she make the girl understand that she couldn't go back? She didn't know how to go back. She was afraid to go back and be happy again.

Then, like a gust of wind in her face, she realized she'd forgotten how to be happy. She'd been happy until her parents had been killed, and then with David, she was truly happy again. But when she'd seen his eyes when he looked at Carissa all those years ago, she knew he was gone. At least she'd assumed as much.

Tears burned her eyes. She squeezed them shut and took a deep breath. Her eyes shot open when she heard Carissa's voice.

"Hi, are you the real estate agent for this house?" she asked the woman who had just locked the front door and put the key back in the lock box on the doorknob.

"Yes, Sally Foster."

Sally walked down the three small steps and toward

them.

"Carissa Kendal," she introduced herself and held her hand out to meet Sally's. "This is Sophia Burkhalter."

"Sophia Burkhalter, the cellist?" Sally's eyes opened wide when Sophia nodded and extended her hand. "It's an honor to meet you. My husband is from Italy, and Pablo DiAngelo is one of his favorite hometown people."

"He'd be honored."

"Were you looking at the house?"

"We'd love to see it." Carissa's enthusiastic reply had Sophia opening her mouth to contradict. "Can we make an appointment with you?"

"Actually my other clients who are interested in the house just left, but I could take you in if you'd like. It's vacant and available immediately."

Sophia clenched her teeth, but Carissa smiled and laced her arm through Sophia's.

"We'd really appreciate that." Carissa drew Sophia along as Sally started back up the walk.

The exterior was just as Sophia had remembered it. Each house, though similar to the others on the street, had its own personality. It might have been a tree or a plant, but in Sophia's eyes, they'd always looked different. The brick porch still held its character, and the large oak door was the same.

Sophia held her breath as Sally unlocked the door and stepped inside.

"You can do this," Carissa said as she pulled her through the door.

Standing in the entryway, Sophia felt at home for the first time in ten years. The tears that had been burning her eyes earlier were finally falling, and she silently cursed the Warrior in her for not wearing her scarf to wipe them before someone saw them.

Carissa noticed the tears. "Are you okay?" she whispered.

Sophia could only nod.

The hardwood floor was still in good shape. She smiled when she thought of the hours of sanding and staining that she'd put into that floor. It was a blessing to see it looking so nice.

"The carpets need to be replaced in the bedrooms, but that's something most people want to do anyway." Sally started through the house.

The mantel and the fireplace looked the same, but the window coverings were different. Sophia thought she actually liked them better than the ones she had chosen so many years earlier.

"The kitchen cabinets have been updated as well as the appliances." Sally opened the back door, and the three of them stood on the small cement porch. "The previous owners added a retractable awning, which is wonderful for outdoor entertaining. They also ran the gas to the outside for a grill hookup."

Back in the house, Sophia poked her head into the guest bathroom and smiled when she saw her small rosebud wallpaper still hanging. It had been the last thing she'd changed in the house before she'd left.

"Why don't we take a look around the upstairs," Sally said as she started up the staircase that Sophia already knew would lead to the three bedrooms above them.

She swallowed hard. She wasn't sure she wanted to see where she and David had made love so many times and where they'd planned their life.

Taking a deep breath of courage, she walked up the stairs behind Carissa.

"Oh, isn't that sweet?" Carissa placed her hand on her chest as she walked into the bedroom at the top of the stairs.

Sophia followed and then wished she hadn't. It was a nursery for a baby girl. The walls were pink with painted murals of fairy tales. The tears were falling again.

"Please excuse me." Sophia backed into the hallway and to the bathroom across the hall. She shut the door and stood looking into the mirror. She'd looked into that mirror so many times before, only that face had been younger and full of hope. The face she wore now was full of worry and self-pity.

When she emerged, she could hear Carissa and Sally downstairs again. "Take your time," Sally called up.

Disgusted with herself for acting so childishly, Sophia took a deep breath and walked down the hall to the master bedroom where she'd slept and woke in David's arms. This room, too, was the same as it was ten years earlier. Relief washed over her.

"What do you think?" Carissa was in the doorway.

"This was quite a shock to the system. It wasn't what I had in mind for today."

"If you and dad worked things out, you'd need a place to live."

"I have a place to live. I live in Seattle," she reminded her.

Carissa turned her lips up into a crooked grin that Sophia had seen many times on her father's face. "And does Seattle feel like home?"

Again, her stomach tightened. Nowhere had felt like home—until she'd crossed the threshold of the house with Carissa.

CHAPTER EIGHT

They'd blown off their cello rehearsal, and Sophia feared the wrath of Pablo even though he wasn't near. He'd threatened to kick her out of his ensemble if she slacked on her practice while away. She hadn't taken his threats seriously, but it should have been enough to make her stick to a schedule. He'd done it to other musicians.

They'd gone to the chick flick, as promised, and eaten through two buckets of popcorn while trying to hold in the tears between laughs. Afterward, they went to the Juice Emporium and treated themselves to a cold, fruity blend of whatever Mary Alice chose to make for them.

Mary Alice wiped up the counter and looked at Carissa. "Hey, kiddo, will you cover the counter for ten minutes while I gossip with Sophie?"

"Sure."

Mary Alice joined Sophia at one of the tables. "I'm very happy to see the two of you out and about together. She really has needed a woman in her life. One that wasn't doped up all the time."

"I don't know that I'm in her life very much. I leave in a week."

Mary Alice nodded. "Well, at least you've given her a smile."

"What does that mean?"

"She's a sad one," she said, shooting a glance toward Carissa who was helping a customer. "Don't get me wrong. She doesn't walk around moping all the time, but she feels like she's missed out on that normal life so many of us had."

"Had..."

"I didn't mean to bring up bad memories." Mary Alice placed her hand on Sophia's.

"No. I was that girl, too," she said in realization.

"I know that. I was there. That's why I think you two make a great team. You understand her like no one else can." She let out a breath. "Well, I don't want to hook her into working too long. But I did want to invite you and David over for dinner on Sunday night. He'll be back, right?"

Sophia nodded.

"Great. The boys will all be gone and Carissa's working so I know the shop will be taken care of. Seven sharp." Mary Alice patted Sophia's hand and then went back to work.

Sophia sipped her juice. Mary Alice had scammed her into a dinner date—which was just Mary Alice's style. She shook her head. Who *wasn't* in on trying to get her and David back together?

"Okay, so what are we going to do now?" Carissa plopped down in the chair across from Sophia and took a sip of her own drink.

"Let's see. It's eight o'clock on Friday night. You're seventeen years old, and you're spending the evening with a thirty-six-year-old bore." She laughed at herself. "What more could you want to do?"

"Go home and paint our toenails." Carissa bounded from her chair and was out the door before Sophia could even comprehend what she'd said. She waved good-bye to Mary Alice and followed Carissa.

She'd come back to Kansas City planning to leave as soon as the party was over, but she was finding so much that pulled at her to stay.

The smell of popcorn filled the house, even if they

weren't eating much of it after having gorged themselves on it at the movie. The beat of music poured from Sophia's room, and the sound of laughter filtered above it all. Sophia and Carissa sat on the floor, toenails freshly painted and avocado masks covering their faces.

It was eleven o'clock when Katie finally tapped on the door and then pushed it open when it went unanswered.

"Grandma." Sophia peeled the cucumber slices from her eyes. "I'm sorry we woke you."

"Well, we're not used to late nights around here." Her tone was soft as it had always been.

"We're so sorry. We'll turn it down and wrap it up. We didn't realize it had gotten so late." Sophia stood and wobbled to her door. She kissed her gently on the cheek and then wiped off the bit of mask that had transferred to her grandmother's face.

"I love you, Sophie. I'm so happy that you're home."

"I love you, too." She shut the door and wobbled over to the stereo to turn down the music. "Do you know, in all my life, I don't think she ever came to the door to tell me I was too loud at night. I can't remember ever having a slumber party here or friends up here too much. Mary Alice was the only one," she reminisced. "Do you do this a lot?"

"What, makeovers and slumber parties?"

"Yes."

"A few times. My friend Emily...my *old* friend Emily and her mom do this all the time. They let me in on it a few times, but it's kinda their ritual."

Sophia noticed Carissa's eyes divert to the ground behind her green avocado mask. She felt the tears stinging her eyes.

It wasn't sadness in the fact that she hadn't had friends who wanted to paint their toenails with her when she was younger, or the fact that Emily had broken poor Carissa's heart by making out with her boyfriend. At least, this was who Sophia assumed had been part of that. What had saddened her was the fact Carissa had wanted to do such things with her mother and didn't get to. She trusted Sophia to be that mother figure and help her live out her little-girl dreams.

The lump in her throat almost had her gasping for air.

"You know, and I'm not saying I'm going to, but if I were to move back here, we could plan this every few weeks. Just a girls' night in. Old movies, music, popcorn, and toenail polish. We could have a theme," she said, realizing she'd committed without meaning to and was about to go further. "We could choose an OPI color. You know, the ones with the real unique names and then plan the whole night around it."

Carissa looked up at her and smiled. Her eyes had brightened, and Sophia felt the tug at her heart. She'd made her happy.

"I'm going to bed now before Miss Katie grounds us." Carissa stood and pulled the tissues out from between her toes. "My favorite color is An Affair in Red Square. What can we do with that?"

"We'll figure it out."

"How about Friday night next week before the party?"

"It's a date."

Carissa quietly slipped out the door as Sophia's phone rang. It was David's number. She inhaled deeply then answered the phone.

"Hello."

"I'm glad you're up. I was afraid I was going to wake you."

"Carissa and I were having a girls' night."

"What's that?"

"We went to a movie, had a juice, painted our toenails,

put on avocado masks, listened to music, and laughed."

"I can't believe you two are getting along so well. She's always wanted a mother to do those things with."

"That's what she told me. Mandy wasn't that kind of woman?"

"No. No, she certainly wasn't."

Sophia sat down on the edge of her bed. "She calls her Mandy, not Mom."

"She doesn't deserve the title," David repeated the words just as his daughter had done earlier.

"Why did you call me?" Her heart fluttered at the sound of his voice, and she lay back and accepted the wonderful feeling.

"It's hard to lie in your bed and smell you all around me without thinking about you."

"Oh, David." She sat up and raised her hand to her rapidly beating heart. She closed her eyes and thought of the room where he lay. Knowing he was tucked under her sheets in her bed made her long to be there with him.

"I'm sorry, but it's true. How come this is the only furniture in your house?"

"I only ever slept there. I figured the bed should be nice."

"Well, it is. I needed to hear your voice though. It wasn't enough to play the message on your answering machine sixteen times."

"You didn't really do that, did you?" The flutters from her heart moved to her stomach. She missed him more than she ever had.

"Don't believe me? I'm sure your neighbors are not approving of your house guest."

She laughed.

"When are you coming home?"

"Actually, I just got word that my flight out of Chicago

and back to Kansas City will be later."

"They already know that?"

"Yeah. Broken plane, canceled flight, reorganization. It happens. So I should fly in tomorrow night about eleven fifteen."

"Carissa will be sad. She misses you."

"Doesn't sound like it. Sounds like the two of you are happy doing the girl thing."

Sophia sighed, thinking about it. "Yeah, I guess we are."

"Sophie, have you given any thought to what I said to you earlier? You know, about moving back to K.C."

"David, I can't give you positive answers yet."

"I know. I just wondered if you'd thought about it."

Sophia squeezed her eyes tight. "Yes, I've given it some thought." Though she decided not to tell him about seeing the house. She didn't want to fan the flames of an argument she knew she couldn't win.

"Go out with me when I get back? Maybe we could even take a few days and head to Saint Louis or something."

"Why?"

"I've missed you. I think it would be good for us to talk about things."

Sophia sucked in another breath. Her head was filled with images of David lying in her bed, and all she could think was she wanted to be there with him. But she couldn't lead him on. She still had her career to think about. She couldn't just uproot and leave it.

"Mary Alice invited us to dinner on Sunday. Seven o'clock." she said to alter the subject.

"Good. I could use a good meal. Mr. Chan's left me with quite the upset stomach."

"I should have mentioned that, too." She laughed, and

he followed. No matter how much they fought, it seemed like they could fall back into a rhythm, and it only intensified her longing for him.

"Okay, then I'll start with that. It's a date."

"It's a date."

"And I guess I'll see you on Sunday morning. Everyone should be tucked in tight by the time I get home tomorrow."

"David, thanks for stopping by my place. I'll think a bit harder about moving back. I'm at home here, and you're right, I can leave here just as easily as I can leave Seattle when Pablo needs me."

"Thanks for thinking of it." But his voice had an edge it hadn't carried earlier.

Sophia woke up too late for breakfast Saturday, and Carissa had already taken Katie and Millie to the grocery store so the house was empty. She made herself a cup of coffee and a piece of toast and headed to the study to work on her music. It was well after lunch when she emerged to find herself still alone. A note on the study door informed her Carissa was working and the older ladies were out visiting.

By two o'clock, she was fidgeting with nervous energy. She slipped into a pair of yoga pants and a T-shirt from a Pablo DiAngelo tour of France, found a water bottle with the logo of David's airline on it, and then headed out the door with no goal other than walking far enough to calm herself. She passed her elementary school and the post office. She passed the office her grandfather had worked at until he retired and the grocery store where Katie shopped. Before she knew it, she'd walked three miles in one direction. All the way to Cherry Street.

What the hell, she thought. She could look at the house

one more time. It wasn't as if she was really going to buy it, but she could remember it.

"Sophia?" The unmistakable voice of the neighbor from across the street rang in her ears as she turned around to see Mrs. Crow scooting toward her with the help of her walker. "Is that you?"

"Yes, Mrs. Crow, it's me. How are you?" She had her hand already extended toward the elderly woman, who had finally made it across the street.

"Where have you been? I've missed you."

"I've been touring the world, Mrs. Crow. You're looking very well."

"Oh, this old hip of mine," she sighed. "Well, I could go on for days. So, you lookin' at the house? It hasn't been the same since you two young kids lived there."

Sophia laughed at the young kids comment. Surely, the old lady hadn't thought of them like that, but then again, she and David weren't much more than kids when they bought the house.

"Carissa and I looked through it the other day. I'm thinking about moving back, and my own house seems like a good place to start. Not to mention, I did most of the fix-it-up work in there."

"It would be a good investment. Carissa, that's that little girl?"

"Yes. She's David's daughter. She's seventeen now."

"And that woman?"

Sophia swallowed back the resentment that Mrs. Crow knew *that woman*. And that *that woman* had lived in her home.

"She left them. David has raised Carissa alone."

Mrs. Crow just nodded. "Well, you should buy the house. I'd love to have you back. I have grape jelly in jars, and I'll have one on your porch when you sign."

"Well I don't know…"

"You do. Nice to see you, Sophia." The woman turned back toward her house. "See you soon."

The encounter with Mrs. Crow reminded Sophia more than ever how much she'd enjoyed the feeling of friends and community here in Kansas City. But did she really want to move back? She broke into a jog to clear her mind.

A few steps later, her cell phone vibrated in her pocket. It was a text message from Carissa.

CAN WE TALK?

What could Carissa's text mean? If it weren't urgent, Sophia was sure she'd have waited until she got home. Her jog turned into a run. Soon she was in front of the Juice Emporium and she ducked inside, her face damp with perspiration and her blood pumping wildly through her veins.

"Sophia, hi!" Carissa smiled from behind the counter. She'd pulled her hair away from her face in a ponytail and wore a hint of makeup in muted colors. The days of blackened eyes seemed to be gone, replaced by a happier-looking teenager. "What are you doing?"

"I just got your text."

"I didn't mean you had to come right now." She let out a laugh.

"I was already out running." Sophia wished she were more in tune with Carissa.

"Why?"

"I meant to go for a walk. That was two hours ago. I ended up on Cherry Street, and Mrs. Crow came out and told me she had grape jelly for me."

"You went back to the house?" Carissa's voice rose in pitch, and her eyes grew wide with her smile.

Sophia shook her head. "I just ended up there. It

doesn't mean anything."

"Can I get you something?"

"I'd really, really, really like a cup of water."

"I can do that." Carissa turned around to get the water and then back to Sophia. "Mary Alice says you're going to her house tomorrow night for dinner with Dad."

"Yes. He's happy to have a good, home-cooked meal. And since he was stuck in my apartment with bad Chinese food, I guess I owe him that." She sipped the water. It was refreshing, like being home with family, and she sighed. "Millie says you're headed over to Emily's to fix things up. Will you be okay?"

"Yeah. I'm really mad at her, and I just want to talk out what happened with her and that jerk and get the story straight. She owes me an apology, and I expect to get it and the full story. It's the missing parts in life that make things all crazy."

The statement zeroed in on the truth, and Sophia couldn't form a response right away. She could only wish she'd been as wise as the young woman who stood before her.

"I guess I'd better head home." She drank down her water and threw the cardboard cup into the trash. "Good luck with Emily."

"Thanks."

"What time do you think you'll be home?"

"I don't know, but shouldn't be later than nine. I really need some beauty sleep." She knit her brows. "I did want to ask you something. That's why I texted you. I audition for first chair on Wednesday. Would you be there?"

The very question had Sophia gasping at breath. "At your audition? Are you sure? That's nerve-racking enough."

"I think it would be fine. I'd love to have you."

Sophia smiled. Pride flowed through her and a joy like

she'd never known. "I would love to be there for you."

Sophia sank onto the front steps of her grandmother's house. As her breathing and pulse slowed, she contemplated what Carissa had said to her at the juice shop. How could it be that the little girl she'd run away from was the one that had so much wisdom? Sophia reached for her neck. There was no scarf there, only the necklace her mother had given her and the scar that she'd hidden for so many years that really wasn't so bad.

Warrior, she thought. How different would her life have been if she'd waited David out and not been so afraid of what had happened? She combed her fingers through her sweaty curls and gave it some serious thought. How horrible it all must have been for him. To find out he had a daughter and then the woman he loved left him without explanation. She was woman enough to realize that was only the start. Carissa couldn't have been in the very best of ways when she banged on their door that day. How frightened must she have been?

Sophia thought of the little girl who'd looked lost and deserted. She was dirty, and her clothes were torn. For seven years she'd lived with that woman she wouldn't even call her mother. What horrors had she witnessed in those seven years? It was no wonder she'd searched out her father.

What would it have been like not to know your father? Sophia had known her father, and she'd loved him and he had loved her. He'd read her stories and sang her songs while she sat cuddled on his lap. He had taught her to tie her shoes and ride a bike. Every night he'd tucked her into bed and told her he loved her. Not only did he love her, he loved her mother, too. One thing that she would never forget was the way they would look at each other and the way they would look at her. It had been devastating to lose them both. But never to have known them, or even one of them, that was unthinkable.

Then there was Mandy. Who was she really? Sophia surely would like to know. How had David come to know this woman and father her child? From the few things she'd learned about Mandy, they weren't the kind of people that would ever have hooked up. But, obviously, they had.

These were all things she should have hung around and asked, rather than running away and staying away for ten years because she assumed she'd been pushed out of the picture. From what Carissa had told her, she'd never been out of the picture.

When her grandmother found her on the porch and said that she and Millie were going to the neighbor's for dinner, she was grateful.

"You should come with us," Katie offered.

"Oh, thank you. I really think I'd like a night in," Sophia politely refused.

"Okay then. There are some leftovers in the fridge."

"Thank you."

Katie patted Sophia's shoulder as she passed by her.

"He'll be home soon," she said softly as she walked into the house.

CHAPTER NINE

At ten o'clock, Sophia shut herself in her room and paced the floor.

She'd phoned Pablo three times. There was still no answer to her phone calls or to the fate of her career, which lay in his hands at the moment.

She looked out the window of her room and saw David's car in the driveway. She scrubbed her hands over her face and through her hair before turning to her desk and sitting down. She opened her laptop and searched for his flight. It was expected around eleven-thirty. Throwing her head back, she took a deep breath.

"If I hurry, I can catch him," she whispered to herself. "I love him."

She'd said it aloud—admitted it to herself without hesitation. She grabbed her purse and raced down the stairs.

The house was quiet. Everyone had turned in for an early night. Out of courtesy, she wrote a note and laid it on the kitchen table.

Gone to pick up David. Will be back soon. Sophia.

Her hands began to tremble as she backed out of the driveway. What would she say to him? What would he think of her being there? She couldn't think about it. She just had to do it.

She found a parking space and began to run through the parking garage and into the building. It was eleven fifty when she reached the furthest point she could go without a ticket.

For a moment, she thought of how he'd followed her off the plane. The path he had taken. She read the monitors and looked for the gate and the luggage carousel, though he'd have his with him. He'd only gone to the luggage carousel because he'd been following her. Her heart was pounding in her chest. Had she missed him? How would she find him? She hadn't given it much thought. How would he know she...

"Sophie?"

She spun to see him, his luggage to his side, his cap tucked up under his arm. Her lower lip quivered as she walked to him. His eyes were light with sheer joy that she was there. The smile that crossed his lips told her that he missed her. When he dropped his hat and scooped her up in his arms, she knew he still loved her.

Not one word passed between them before he crushed his mouth to hers, and she pulled him tighter. Her fingers wound in his hair as his hands held the small of her back. She parted her lips and deepened the kiss. Her head spun, her knees grew weak, and she couldn't let go. She didn't want to let go. Never again. He was hers. He'd always been hers, and she knew he'd waited for her to return. She knew it all just from the power of his kiss.

"Sophie, I love you. I've always loved you." He kissed her again.

She wasn't sure her feet were on the ground, and her head kept spinning when he pulled back to rest his forehead against hers. "What are you doing here?"

"I missed you. I couldn't be without you one more minute. I've missed too many of them," she admitted breathlessly as she touched his face and breathed him in. "David, I love you, too. I've never stopped loving you."

"It's been a damn long time to love someone and not have them." He pulled her close again. "Sophie, never leave me again."

"I promise I won't." She wrapped her arms tightly

around his neck and held him against her.

"C'mon." He grabbed her hand and his suitcase. "Where did you park?"

"I don't know. Over there, I think," she said laughing as he pulled her along.

Once they found the car, he threw his suitcase in the trunk, and each of them climbed in as quickly as they could. The instant the doors closed, he had Sophia's face in his hands, her mouth pressed to his, and her hands on his chest. That was how it should have always been, she thought.

"You're sleeping in my arms tonight," he muttered against her lips.

"Yes."

"I want to make love to you."

"Yes."

His mouth smiled against hers, and he started the car. "This is going to be the longest drive home."

They drove from the airport enfolded in intimate silence. David squeezed her hand, holding it tighter, and she'd smile that smile he'd fallen in love with so many years earlier.

He'd been right. It was the longest drive.

The moment they reached the house, each of them flew from the car and into each other's arms. The night was dark except for a few stars that spotlighted them in the driveway.

David held her tight to him, his hand tangled in her hair. He pulled her closer to him, placing kisses on her cheeks, her forehead, and then gently on her lips.

"You're shaking. Are you cold?" he whispered.

"No. I'm nervous."

"It's not like we haven't done this before." He grazed a kiss over her lips.

"I haven't…well, you were…"

David took her by the shoulders and eased her back to look her in the eyes. "You haven't made love to another man since you left?"

She took a deep breath and swallowed hard. "David, you're the only man I've ever been with."

"But Pablo?"

She shook her head. "I may have tried to replace you with him, but our relationship was never like that. Pablo has never been my lover."

Her words tugged at his heart.

"I thought…"

"I know what you thought." She touched his face. "You're the only man I've ever loved, the only one I've shared myself with."

He pulled her closer, feeling her body tremble against his. "I'll take care of you. It's all I've ever wanted to do. For us to be a family."

"I know." She lifted her head and met his eyes. "I'm sorry."

He put his finger over her lips to stop her. He wasn't ready for conversation. Not now. He needed to hold her, to love her, to feel her once more.

With a playful smile, he pulled her by the hand to the back door.

He took her mouth with his, feeding the fire burning deep inside of him. With their arms locked around each other, they stumbled through the kitchen and crept up the stairs to her room.

It was dark except for the cascade from the street lamp outside her window.

David wandered kisses over her face and down her slender neck. His name was a whisper on her lips, and it drove him wild. He could have her dress off her in a heartbeat, but he wanted to caress her and hold her until she had completely melted.

Her skin was just as he'd remembered it. Soft and scented of rose petals. Her pulse pounded beneath his lips as he placed kisses down her throat.

He skimmed his hands up her sides, reached behind her neck, and slowly opened the zipper to her dress. He slid the soft, cotton material from her shoulders and watched as it pooled in the lamplight at her feet. Her body was exposed, and he felt her tense under his touch.

He stood still for a moment, waiting for her to relax, wanting her to savor every moment of their lovemaking. She took a little breath and then unbuttoned his shirt, the soft light turning her features to molten gold. She slid her hands under the fabric and over his skin, and his own heart hammered in his chest.

Moving slowly, he unhooked her bra and let it fall to the ground atop the discarded dress. Beneath his hands, he felt her shudder as he touched the scar on her throat then gently he kissed it.

"I love you," he whispered. "I love everything about you." He kissed her neck and, inch by sweet inch, worked his lips down her breast and took the tip into his mouth.

Sophia gripped her fingers in his hair. He knew she hadn't felt the heat that vibrated through her since his mouth had last trailed over her body, and he wanted to make it special for her. She arched against him as his hands slid across her skin. It wasn't going to be easy to hold back.

He pulled her toward the bed, covering her mouth with his once more. Would he ever get enough of the taste of her? He lowered her to the cool sheets, then unbuttoned his pants and slid them to the floor. Her unwavering eyes captivated his.

Sophia was back, and she was back for good. She'd

never let him touch her if she hadn't planned on staying. That's how Sophia was.

With gentle fingers, he pulled the silk panties down her legs. He drank in the sight of her body. It was still perfect. His body quickly reacted as he lowered his body next to hers and focused on her, and not his own burning needs. He touched her skin with his fingers. The scar that ran from under her arm to the top of her hip had his attention as he ran a gentle touch down her side. With kisses just as tender, he kissed her stomach, crossing over the scar that ran from side to side. He'd never been afraid of her scars. What could have been had always caused more fear in him. What would life ever have been for them all without Sophia in it?

He shifted and rose above her. He felt her tremble, but only a moment later, her hands roamed down his back.

"David…" Her whisper of his name drove him mad as he slid inside her. She moved against him.

God, he could lose himself right there. He wanted to take her. He wanted to plunge against her in a violent storm, washing away the ten years he'd missed of kissing her, touching her, and loving her. But he needed to be gentle with her.

"Sophie. I've missed you. I've missed this." His kiss heated against her mouth, and she moaned against his lips. "I haven't touched another soul since you," he whispered in her ear as her fingers dug into his skin. "I haven't wanted to. It's always been you. Only you."

"David." The quiver in her voice told him she was spilling over. He'd driven her to the very edge where heaven and earth melded together and the sky spun. He felt her shudder beneath him, and a moment later, he tumbled with her.

Breathless, he fell against her damp body. Their chests

heaved, their hearts pounding out the same rhythm.

"Marry me." The words flew from his mouth as he breathed in the scent of her beneath him.

Sophie gasped, and he covered her mouth with his to stifle any answer she may give him. He didn't want the answer. He wanted to live, right where he was, in the moment…for the rest of his life.

It was past seven when he watched her eyes flutter open.

"Good morning." He kissed her on the mouth. Her lips were soft, full, and warm, and he lingered over them before pulling back to enjoy the play of sunlight in her hair.

"Good morning." Sophia bit her lip. "We didn't think this through, did we?"

"What's that?"

"You should have left my room hours ago." Panic filled her voice. "What are they going to think?"

"Why should you care what they think? I'm forty. I can sleep in the bed of a woman if I want to."

"Oh, David!" Covering her body, she shot up. "This just isn't some fling. My grandmother is downstairs. Your aunt is downstairs. Your daughter." She covered her mouth. "Oh, God! She's next door. What if she heard us?"

"We were quiet." He smiled as he ran his finger down her bare arm.

"This is horrible."

"It was not," he teased.

"Oh, David." Sophia slapped his hand away. "You have to get out of here before anyone finds out."

"Let them find out." He pulled her back to him and wrapped his arms around her tightly. "Make love to me again. This time the sun is up, and I can see you."

"David…" He stopped her protest as he rolled her over

and made love to her one more time.

Another hour passed before David decided it was time for them to make their appearance downstairs.

"Why don't you get in the shower? If they think something is going on up here, they'll hear the water and not pay any more attention. I'll sneak out and head down the hall."

Sophia lazily shook her head with a satisfied smile. She wrapped her arms around his neck and pressed her naked body against his once more.

"I can't believe what we've done."

"I've waited ten years to wrap my arms around you again. Trust me, this isn't just a one-time thing. I plan to do this a lot more." He kissed her forehead and turned her around, sending her toward the shower.

He collected his uniform and laid it out on the bed. There were two weeks before he had to go back. The thought had him smiling. Not only did he not have to work, he had Sophia. The time he had off was going to be exclusively hers.

As he pulled on his pants, he thought about what he'd said to her just after he made love to her. He'd asked her to marry him again. What had he been thinking? As he picked up his shirt and draped it over his arm, he realized he hadn't been thinking. He'd been feeling. His heart knew what it was he wanted most.

What he wanted was Sophia Burkhalter as his wife. Finally.

When he heard the water running, he opened the bedroom door and stepped out quietly. He shut it behind him and turned right into Carissa.

Her eyes grew wide as she saw him. He stood with his uniform shirt draped over his arm, shoes in his hand, chest bare, and his hair rumpled.

A knot formed in his stomach as he stared at his daughter. Oh, they'd had the talk. The you-really-should-be-married-before-you-make-love-to-someone talk. Now he stood face-to-face with her, and a heat rose in his cheeks.

She grinned.

God, could a grown man die of embarrassment? Sophia was right. He should have left in the wee hours of the morning. Perhaps he shouldn't have been in her room at all. That thought was fleeting. He'd risk death by embarrassment, or firing squad, to make love with her just once.

"Good morning, Dad." Carissa walked closer to him, her smile still wide on her lips.

"Good morning, sweetheart." Any other day he would kiss her on the cheek, but his feet froze in place.

"Flight get in really late?" She was inching toward him, her arms crossed over her chest—smirking.

"Yes. Sophie picked me up." His voice caught.

Carissa nodded. "Yeah, I thought she might if I got home early enough for her to have the car."

His daughter was such a thoughtful person it made his chest hurt.

"I missed you, Dad. I'm glad you're home." Carissa rose on her toes and kissed her father on his unshaven cheek. Then she ran her hand over the stubble of whiskers. "Better get showered and shaved." She smiled again and let out a little laugh. "Mmmm, you smell like roses."

Sophia applied her lip gloss and gave herself a once-over in the mirror. She'd struggled with the decision of even putting on makeup. For the first time in a long time, she hadn't seen a need. She was glowing from the inside, and she'd never felt so satisfied.

The sundress she chose she'd bought in Italy. She slipped it over her head. Then she reached for her Saint Nicholas medal and fastened it around her neck. She took a long look at herself and smiled. For a brief moment, she had to study herself extra close. The scar seemed to have faded. It was nonsense, she knew, but now in her eyes it wasn't as big as it once had been.

That's how it had always been when she was with David. Her scars and bad feelings didn't exist when he was around—when he loved her. A smile crossed her lips, and her heart beat a little faster.

She closed her eyes and thought about last night. It was as though not a day had passed since he'd touched her. The memories of those feelings were so close. Then her eyes shot open.

He'd asked her to marry him.

Panic flooded her again. Surely he couldn't have meant it. She'd been back in his life only a week. She'd be gone in another week.

Sophia lifted her hand to her chest, hoping to calm her rapidly beating heart.

She'd be gone and away from him…unless she bought the house on Cherry Street. She could do it. She'd never done anything with the money she'd earned while touring with Pablo. He'd seen to it that all her expenses on tour were always paid. Her only expense was her apartment in Seattle, and that truly had never been much of an expense.

Her palms grew moist, and she rubbed them on the skirt of her dress. The house could be hers. But what about the house David was building for himself and Carissa? What about Carissa? She couldn't assume that just because he'd said the words and they'd made love one night, he really wanted to marry her. Perhaps he'd changed. Perhaps she had, too. What would happen if they found out they weren't compatible anymore? Perhaps they weren't compatible with Carissa. The only time she'd been around both of them together she was flinging insults as fast as the seventeen-year-old.

She walked back to her bed and sat down. She let out a long breath and took a moment to sort out her thoughts. If she gave into the what–ifs, she'd need to leave Kansas City immediately and return to Seattle or Italy. Perhaps if she gave it at least the rest of the week, she'd have a better grasp on things. Just perhaps, it would work out for them—all of them. After all, he'd asked her to stay, and Carissa had seen to it she'd known that her old house was for sale.

It was a lot to think about.

David heard Sophia's door shut and her feet pad on the stairs as he reached for the knob to his door. He stepped back. He'd give her a moment to arrive before he did.

Guilt plagued him. She'd walk into a room full of people who knew they'd made love last night, and his daughter would surely be among those with smug faces. He realized he'd been cowering in his room behind the door, waiting for her. He'd danced, and now it was time to pay the band.

Slowly, he made his way down the stairs. The house was quiet. How could four women be so silent when there was gossip?

He turned the corner to the kitchen and saw her there. She stood in front of the window, a cup of coffee in her hand, looking out over the yard. She was alone.

David slid up behind her and wrapped his arms around her waist. Leaning into him, she rested her head against his chest and closed her eyes.

He brushed his lips against her neck, pausing between kisses to ask, "Did you run everyone off?"

"No one was here. And it's only seven forty-five."

"Where did they all go?"

She turned in his arms and looked up at him, her expression mystified. "I don't know. There wasn't a soul around."

"Carissa?"

"Not here, and neither is your car."

"She didn't say anything this morning when I saw her." The words slipped through his lips, and he frowned when he realized he hadn't intended to tell her about that.

"You saw her?" The worry on her face had him wishing he could bite back his words.

"Yes. Ran right into her as I left your room. I tell you, I haven't felt that little since I was a child."

"Oh, God." She walked away from him. "She heard us, didn't she? She knows what we were doing."

Sophia sat down at the table and buried her face in her hands.

"She didn't hear us. But, yes, I think she has a pretty good idea of what was going on. She's seventeen. We've talked about sex." He sat down next to her and took her hand in his as she lifted her head. "She loves you. She called me and texted me the whole time I was gone. She loved every moment with you. You're the first mother figure she's had around that seems to have made a good impact on her life.

He kissed her fingers.

"I told you, she's a good kid. She's very smart, and I promise you, had she heard us or been bothered by my making love to you last night, I surely would have heard about it. You may have noticed Carissa holds no punches."

Sophia took her free hand and ran it through his hair,

then rested it on his cheek.

"I love you."

"And I love you." He kissed the palm of her hand.

"I love your daughter, too."

"You know, she's still young enough to adopt." He smiled, but Sophia's lips pursed. "Sophie, I didn't mean to…"

"David…about last night…about what you said."

"No. Don't go there now." He stood and paced the kitchen. "It's there. You know how I feel, and you know what I want. When you're ready to commit or ready to run, let me know. But for now, I have you for seven more days. Carissa has her audition Wednesday. We go through the new house on Thursday and approve everything before closing. Saturday is the party for the women, and Sunday, before you fly away from me, I'm going to make love to you for hours. Then you can tell me your answers to all the crazy things I have asked and will ask."

She nodded, but worry filled her eyes, and he hated that part.

"Okay, now I'm starving. We don't have a car, but the sun is shining and it's a beautiful August morning. What do you say we hit an old favorite and walk down to The Spot for breakfast?"

"They're still in business?"

"Sure are. Even expanded to ten tables. And, of course, they still have Betsy serving at the counter."

"Wouldn't be The Spot without her."

David offered her his hand, and she stood. He gathered her into his arms and pulled her close.

"You know, maybe they left us here alone on purpose. Maybe they want us to make love all day without being interrupted." He raised his eyebrows suggestively, and she laughed.

"We'd better get breakfast. Besides as soon as that little girl of yours gets home, we have to practice."

"Damn." He gave her bottom a playful smack. "I'll always be second to that cello, won't I?"

The diner was just as she'd remembered with its metal siding and neon lights. The only change was the tables around the walls. David escorted her to a corner booth where they could be alone.

Betsy had tears in her eyes when she pulled Sophia from the booth and wrapped her large arms round her.

"I thought you'd never come back. I missed you, kiddo."

"I missed you, too." They chatted for a minute before Betsy returned to her duties. Everyone had missed Sophia, and it warmed her heart.

David spread jelly on his toast.

"Aren't you hungry?"

"You'd think I would have worked up an appetite, but…"

"Ah, after-sex breakfast just isn't the same ten years later?"

"David!" She looked around to see that no one heard him, but he was laughing. "I just have a lot on my mind, I guess."

She pushed around the eggs on her plate.

"So, tell me about your new house," she finally said, lifting a forkful of eggs to her mouth.

"Well, it's nice, but I'm having second thoughts about moving into it."

"Really?" She set down her fork. "Why?"

"When we decided to build it, Carissa was only a sophomore. We toyed with the idea, found the area, picked out the layout, and by the time they broke land, she was a junior. It took longer than I thought." He sipped his coffee. "She'd been having some problems at school. I told you about the counselor." Sophia nodded. "Well, that same counselor moved from the middle school to the high school and was continuing to give her problems, so the initial thought was it was best to move and change schools. The new house is thirty minutes from your grandmother's.

"Then as soon as we broke ground, that counselor changed schools again. Now, if Carissa stays at the school she's at, she'll be commuting an hour a day. With the opportunities coming at her with orchestra and her being elected to the student council, I just can't see pulling her out and moving her. But I don't want her commuting either. Then there's the fact that I'm still gone eight to ten days out of the month. I don't know why it didn't cross our minds when we picked out the house. Desperate to move on, I guess."

Sophia's head spun. He was adding more things to the mix that she was being forced to think about. Suddenly the house they were building didn't seem to be a problem. If she bought the house on Cherry Street, they could live together as a family.

Family. Did she really understand the meaning of the word? She'd been a little girl when she lost her family. Her grandparents had been her only family. Carissa had never really had that storybook family, and David...well, he was the only one with a real grasp on that. His mother and father lived only a few states away, lapping up the sun in the Gulf of Mexico in their dream retirement home.

She remembered the comment he'd made about adopting Carissa. Would Carissa really want that?

Every word she'd said about having and wanting a relationship with a mother was flooding through Sophia's head.

They had a theme to paint their toenails OPI colors and watch movies. If she moved back, they could have it all. They could *be* a family. Carissa could still go to school and have a mother. She could be Carissa's mother! David could keep traveling, and Carissa would have someone at home to take care of her.

She could still play. Her career as a professional cellist didn't have to end. She'd traveled the world. Maybe it was time to settle down and play for the symphony or even a local orchestra. Maybe she could teach.

And she and David could finally be together.

Sophia dropped her fork to her plate, snapping her from her trance.

"Are you okay?" David reached for her hand.

She nodded. After all the years of heartache, it seemed too good to be true. She couldn't tell him. Not yet. "I think I should get back and practice before we go to Mary Alice and Jeremy's for dinner."

They began their walk back to the house, hand in hand. Their route took them past Cherry Street, and Sophia knew David had guided her that direction on purpose.

When he headed toward the block with the house they had shared, she stopped on the corner.

"Don't do this," she pleaded.

"Do what?" David gathered her in his arms and pulled her close to him.

"My head is spinning with all the things going on in it. Do we really need to walk down memory lane? Literally?"

"I didn't realize it would bother you." His eyes were sad. She hadn't meant to hurt him. But she'd barely had a chance to get used to the idea that they might be a family again. What if she was wrong? She didn't want to build up his hopes for nothing.

"I'm sorry." She took his hands in hers and took a cleansing breath. "I've already been down this street twice. It's hard enough to see it, but to know it's empty and…"

"What do you mean it's empty?"

Her eyes shifted to his. He didn't know.

"The house…it's empty and for sale."

The darkness in his eyes deepened. He'd said it himself—he wasn't sure about the house they were building. Sophia knew the moment he had the thought that they could move back to Cherry Street.

"Let's just go home." She laced her arm though his.

"Yeah. Let's go home."

The word *home* echoed in the silence between them.

The moment they walked through the door of her grandmother's house, Sophia went straight for the study while David raced up the stairs to his room two at a time.

She dug through her purse and searched for Sally's card. She was sure she'd tucked it in there just in case she decided she might want to look at the house again.

Finally, she dumped the contents on the desk and frantically pawed through the items. She found the card tucked between the pages of her date book. She pulled out her cell phone and dialed.

"Good morning. This is Sally Foster." The cheerful voice on the other end sent a bolt of panic racing through Sophia.

"Sally, this is Sophia Burkhalter, I met—"

"Sophia! Oh, my husband was so impressed when I told him I showed you a house the other day."

"Well, thank you, but—"

"So, what did you think? It's lovely, isn't it?"

"Well, yes, and I—"

"It's very popular, too."

"It is?" Sophia's voice dipped.

"Well, yes. The people who looked at it the same day as you and your daughter…" Sophia bit back the correction. "They've been back twice, and I think they'll make an offer. And I just got off the phone with another gentleman who says he'd like to see the house for him and his daughter. He's lived in the neighborhood and would like to move back." Sally's voice was too chipper, and Sophia knew for sure that man was David.

"You're showing him the house then?"

"Yes. I'm on my way over there right now, in fact. He seemed very anxious."

"I'll bet he did." Sophia heard the front door slam. Her heart pounded in her chest. But what if David wasn't the man Sally had spoken to? What if someone else bought that house…bought her and David's home?

"Sally, I'll be staying in the Kansas City area, and I'd like to buy the house."

CHAPTER TEN

David stood outside the house he and Sophia had shared. The rose bushes he'd planted in front of the porch still held the blooms on them in the late summer heat. He smiled. He'd planted them on the anniversary of having the house for a year. Sophia had had a tree planted in the yard to honor her parents. It was much larger now, and in another ten years, it could hold a tree house. Oh, wouldn't it be wonderful if together they could make it their home again, but this time with a family.

Carissa was young yet. She needed a family. She needed her father, and dammit, she needed a mother. Sophia was only thirty-six. She could still have children. The children she'd desperately wanted. They could adopt an entire houseful if she wanted. God, he wanted to give it all to her. He wanted to give the world to both of them.

A car pulled up behind him. Must be the real estate agent, he thought. He turned and waited for the driver to exit, but the warm smile that he'd held on his lips faded when Mandy slid out of the car. The muscles in the back of his neck knotted.

"What in the hell are you doing here?"

"I followed you from that old lady's house."

"What the hell are you doing here?" Heat was rising in his cheeks, and his heart was racing. Just looking at the woman made him want to break something. He shoved his hands into his pockets and clenched them into fists.

Mandy stood silently for a moment behind the car door. She raised her chin.

David looked at her more closely. She'd cleaned up. He could see that she was clean and sober, but not healthy. Her blonde hair, pulled back in a ponytail, was dull. Her skin was pale, and her blue eyes were sunken. She looked sick, fragile, and old, but, for the first time, not strung out.

"Mandy, I asked you, what the hell…"

"David, I want to see my daughter."

"*My* daughter. You gave her up," he reminded her fiercely.

"I want to make sure she's okay."

"She's fine." His retort was short and quick. "What the hell—"

"I need you." Her voice trembled.

"You left. You don't need me. I don't have anything to offer…"

She moved from behind the car door, revealing her swollen belly, and he felt his jaw drop open.

"Yes, I'm pregnant." She ran her hands over her stomach.

He stood silently for a moment, trying to breathe through his anger. "Congratulations?" The word was snide and dripping in disdain for the woman before him.

"I need your help."

"I'm not some stupid, twenty-two-year-old fool you can con with a baby. Go tell your story to whoever knocked you up this time." He turned from her, hoping she'd get back in her car and drive away.

"David." She reached for his arm. "I'm eight months pregnant. I'm much too far along for an abortion, and that wasn't what I wanted anyway."

"Oh, you wanted this baby because the father would support all your habits?"

"Dammit, David, listen! I'm dying. Having this baby will probably kill me."

"Oh, and after all the stellar things you've done to me and Carissa, I'm supposed to believe you?"

"Yes." She laid her hand on his chest.

"Mandy, I have things I need to do." He watched as another car pulled up behind Mandy's, and a professionally dressed blonde stepped from the car and headed his way.

"Mr. Kendal?" She reached out her hand.

"Yes."

"I'm Sally Foster, and you must be Mr. Kendal's fiancée?" She extended her hand and shook Mandy's. "Oh, congratulations on your baby. This will be the perfect house for the two of you. Let's go in, shall we?" She started up the steps.

David's gaze darted to Mandy, whose eyes had widened.

"C'mon, darling, let's go." She seized David's arm and followed Sally up the steps.

He clenched his jaw and shoved his other hand deeper in his pocket.

Sally walked them through the house, giving details as she'd been trained to do. Neither David nor Mandy told her they had lived in the house together years earlier.

"Now this room will be of interest to you both." Sally smiled her glossy smile as she walked them to the nursery. David felt his heart slam into his chest. The pink walls and fairy murals made sweat surface on his brow. Sally talked around them, but David didn't hear her.

"Well, I'll let the two of you look around. I'll wait for you out front." She flashed her smile and left the room.

"Oh, David, the house is still so cute," Mandy gushed. "I always did like this house. I never could see why you sold it. We should have..."

"What the hell, I repeat, what the hell are you doing here?" He spun toward her, looking her square in the eye.

"Why did she think I was your fiancée? She said that like she knew you had one, like she was expecting her to be here with you."

"Mandy, it's no business of yours."

"It is…" she paused and crossed her arms atop her belly, "because I need to know all about it if you're going to raise this baby!"

His eyes were wide as he looked at her in disbelief. He scrubbed his hands over his face and paced the room before finding the calm he needed in order to look at her again.

"I'm sure I didn't hear you correctly. Did you say I was going to raise that baby?"

"That's why I'm here." She moved toward him, but stopped when he backed away from her. "David, I have a heart condition. They said that giving birth to this baby will kill me."

"Women with heart conditions give birth all the time."

"David, I'm different." She ran her hand over her swollen belly. "I'm clean. I swear I'm clean, but all the years…well, my past is killing me. I couldn't abort this baby. I didn't want to. But I won't live to see her."

"Her?"

"Yes, it's a little girl." She smiled, but David turned from her, unable to look at her.

"Where's her father?" He looked out the window at the familiar backyard he'd spent many weekends caring for.

"He doesn't know about her. David, he was a married man that I had a brief affair with. I'm not proud, but now I'm going to have a baby that won't have anyone when I die."

David swallowed hard. "Why me? Why not give her up for adoption?"

"Because she's half of Carissa, too." The words were carefully chosen to pierce David's heart, and they did just that. "Please, David, you've been such a wonderful father to Carissa. This baby needs a father." She reached out to him and touched his arm. "I won't be in the way. I'll be dead."

"And that's supposed to give me comfort?"

She shrugged.

David stood, his eyes still diverted out the window. The air in the room was thick with tension and silence that stretched out for minutes. She'd used Carissa for leverage to get what she wanted before. When it came to Carissa, he'd do anything. And he knew her well enough to know that if she knew she had a sister, she'd want to be part of her life at any cost.

"And if I did this—" He swallowed the lump in his throat. "*If*...what channels would I have to go through?"

"I have you named in my will."

He shook his head, realizing this must have always been her plan. "I'll put you on the birth certificate as her father. Please, David, if you're not part of this, she'll fall into the wrong hands. I mean, you have to be part of this before she's born. Because..." she said on a ragged breath and wiped at the tears that streamed from her eyes, "I'm going to be dead by the time she takes her first breath. David, I'm going to die."

It was more than he could take seeing her cry and her voice shudder. She was baring her soul to him. Her fear was evident in her words and in her eyes. No matter how brave she was trying to be, she was scared of dying. This woman who'd made his life a hell for so many years had also given him Carissa. He gathered her in his arms and pulled her to him.

"David, please give it some thought." She laughed, wiping her cheeks dry with her fingers. "Quickly."

David put his hands on her shoulders and took a long, deep, cleansing breath. "I have to discuss this with Carissa."

Though he didn't know how he'd bring it up to her. Even after saying it, he still wasn't sure he believed he was considering it.

"Of course."

"And Sophia," he added.

"Sophia?" She straightened and pulled from his grip. "The woman downstairs thought I was your fiancée, but your fiancée is Sophia?"

"I've asked her."

"I don't want to know." She stalked out of the room and started down the stairs.

"Mandy!" David ran down the front steps as she opened the door to her car.

"Forget I came. Forget I said anything. The state will get her. Maybe they'll find a nice family for her." Mandy was sobbing as she climbed into the car and sped away.

Sophia's fingers were numb. She'd played for four hours, but it was all she could do to keep her mind focused on what lay ahead for her. After all, she'd told Sally Foster on the phone that she wanted the house and made an offer.

She'd done a lot of thinking as she'd practiced. She'd thought about David and his proposal. He'd asked her to wait to give him all of her answers. She'd wait, but she'd made up her mind. At least, she was sure she'd made up her mind. After too many years, she still wanted to be Mrs. David Kendal.

The back door slammed and feet pounded up the stairs. David was home. Sophia wiped down her cello and slid it into its case.

She looked at her watch. They still had hours until dinner at Mary Alice's. No one else was around. Her pulse tripped. She wanted to be with David.

Slowly, she walked up the stairs. His door was closed.

She could see the light from beneath it and could hear his footsteps. She tapped on the door. He didn't answer right away. Then the door flung open, and he grabbed her by the arm and pulled her into the room, shutting the door behind her.

"David." She couldn't say anything else before his mouth covered hers, and he pushed her up against the door.

His teeth nipped at the tender skin below her ear. He took her breasts in his hands, pressing her nipples roughly between his fingers, and blissful pain shot through her. She dragged her fingers through his hair as he pulled up the skirt of her dress and shoved down her panties.

Somewhere outside, a car door slammed.

"David!" He silenced her again with his mouth. As he caressed her bare skin, her knees went weak. "We...can't..." but her mind was a fog. Her vision blurred. As though a floodgate had lifted, she let herself be immersed in the pleasure of the frantic tempo of his mouth, hands, and body. He pulled her tighter to him, lifted her legs to his waist, and carried her to the bed.

In the time it took her racing heart to beat a handful of times, David had torn off his clothes and was pushing himself deep inside of her.

The rapid pace created spirals of pleasure from her belly to her limbs. A moan vibrated in her throat. His mouth was hot and hungry on her skin. His arms held her so close she could hardly breathe. She felt him shudder as he released and fell still against her.

He didn't move. He didn't speak. Sophia lay still beneath him, listening to him breathe in her ear and feeling the hammering of his heart against her.

"I'm sorry," he whispered in her ear as he lifted his head to kiss her gently.

"Well, we've come a long way in twenty-four hours." She laughed it off as he rolled off her, and she pulled down the skirt of her dress.

"I should have been gentle with you. More considerate. I'd promised you I would."

"David, I'm fine." She sat up and looked down on him. There would be other times, after all. "What's eating at you?"

"Nothing." He rose up on his elbows. "I love you, Sophia. I love you so much." He touched her cheek.

"David, I love you too."

"Let's have a baby."

Sophia smoothed her skirt again. "That's not funny."

"It's not meant to be." He sat up next to her and took her hand. "Marry me, and let's have a baby."

"I can't have a child of my own. You know that!" She broke free of his hand and stood. Tears were stinging her eyes, and she was forcing them back. How could he bring up something so painful?

David reached for his robe, which lay across the foot of the bed, and slipped it on. He took her hands in his and looked her in the eye.

"I do know that. But you're only thirty-six years old. You should have a child like you've always wanted to."

"David, don't you think we should talk about things first? I mean, I've just gotten back. You and I have been in each other's presence exactly four days. And in those four days, we've already said *I love you* to each other, and you've asked me to move back here and marry you. Now you're throwing babies into the equation? What next?"

"Are you saying you don't want children anymore?"

"I'm saying that I gave up on that dream." She looked him over. His hair was damp from the fury he had taken her in, and his dark eyes were sad. "I gave up on a lot of things, David. You were one of them. But here you are."

"Here I am."

"And *if* I marry you, I'll have a daughter. And I actually think she'd accept me."

"I know she'd accept you. What I'm asking is for you to marry me and raise a child with me. One that we name and we stay up all night with. Throw birthday parties for and hold when she's sick. One who we watch take her first steps as we hold out our arms to her. One whose first words are *mama* and *dada*."

"David, you just don't get married and adopt a baby. There are steps. It takes time."

"I know." He blew out a breath. "I'm just saying you deserve that. I deserve that." He gathered her closer. "Think about it. I never got that with Carissa. I want that part too, and I want it with you." He kissed her forehead and rested his cheek against hers. "I know I told you I don't want any answers yet. But let's just say that *if* you do agree to move back, perhaps you'll even consider marrying me. By the way, I'd like that to be quick." He smiled at her and continued, "And let's just say, a child were to bless us. If one landed on our doorstep, would you have a baby with me?"

She studied him closely. There was desperation brewing in his dark eyes. "David, I love you. Why don't we just sit down and talk this entire thing out."

"I want to be very sure you know you'll make me either the happiest man in the world or the saddest."

He pressed a kiss against her lips.

"C'mon. We need a shower."

"David! We can't take a shower in your room. It opens to Carissa's."

"Then we'll take it in yours." He raised his eyebrows playfully. "I'll wash your back."

"God, if my grandmother knew..."

"Oh, Sophie," he said, nipping her lips with a kiss. "I think she knows."

"Gross, David. That's just gross." She turned to let herself out and he pulled her back, holding her tight to him.

"I love you." He smiled at her, his forehead pressed against hers. "Oh! Wait!" He stepped back from her and headed to his dresser. He opened the top drawer and began pushing things from side to side.

"What are you doing?" She laughed as he tore through the drawer.

"Found it." He pulled a box from the drawer and held it toward her.

Sophia's eyes widened.

When David opened the small, black felt box, her lip began to quiver.

"David, that's my ring."

"Yes, it is. And I want you to have it again." He pulled out the princess-cut solitaire and held it in his fingers.

"Oh, I don't know." She shook her head.

"Put it on, Sophie. It's your ring." He reached for her hand and slid the sparkling diamond onto her finger. "Now that looks better."

"David, I can't."

"Just wear it. If you turn me down, we'll discuss who keeps it."

Katie and Millie and David waited for Sophia in the kitchen. She twirled her sundress as she entered the room.

"Do you like it? I got it in Greece."

"You have the most beautiful wardrobe in those two little suitcases," Katie told her.

David moved to her and kissed her right on the mouth in front of Katie and his aunt. It was about time.

Sophia's eyes opened wide, and he smiled. "Just for the record, these two, young ladies think you should move back to K.C. and marry me."

"David," she whispered.

"Oh, Sophia, stop being such an old fuddy-duddy." Katie shook her head as she took flowers from the pile that Millie had cut and then arranged them into the vase before her. "He loves you. You love him." She held up her hand to her granddaughter to stop her argument. "Don't try to deny it. Marry him, and let's forget about the past ten years and move on."

"Grandma." She kissed her on the cheek. "You amaze me."

"I am an amazing woman."

"Yes, you are."

"Well, look at that," Millie added. "You are wearing a very pretty ring."

Katie took Sophia's hand and examined the ring.

"Does this mean you two are completely back together? We can plan a wedding now?"

"It means I've asked, and she'll think about it," David answered, touching Sophia's cheek with his fingertips.

Katie smiled. "Well, that's a start."

"Are you ready?" Sophia asked, shaking her head with a smile.

"Yes. Carissa took the car, and since it's nice out, we might as well walk."

"Sounds lovely." She slipped her hand into his and waved at the women they left behind.

"Well, my dearest friend, I think we accomplished what we set out to do," Katie said as she watched them leave. "I actually think she'll marry him this time."

"I sure hope so." Millie handed Katie another flower. "I'd like to know he was settled down before I die."

"Don't say things like that." Katie took her friend's hand in her own. She noticed how frail Millie looked. She wasn't going to let her start talking about leaving her now.

Hand in hand, their arms swinging between them, David and Sophia walked to Mary Alice and Jeremy Krantz's house.

One glance at David and she knew his mind was working overtime. She wished she could just tell him of her plans. The truth was, though, she wasn't sure what they were exactly. She'd made an offer on the house. She'd called Pablo. She was only waiting for answers from both of them before she made up her mind. Now David had thrown in the possibility of marriage and having a family. She realized her head was working overtime as well.

"What movie do you think about when you hear the word red?"

"What?" His gaze settled on her.

"Just answer the question."

He thought for a moment. "*Hunt for Red October*, I guess."

"Not very girly, is it?"

"I thought all women loved Sean Connery."

"True enough." She gave it some consideration.

"Why?"

"Carissa and I have plans Friday night to paint our toenails An Affair In Red Square and watch a movie with a red theme."

"Oh." He raised her hand to his lips and kissed her fingers. "I don't understand what you just said, but can I come to your party?"

"Absolutely not!" She shook her head. "You'd look ridiculous with red toenails."

"You're probably right." He laughed as they started

down the street where their friends lived. "But, assuming you'll only be down the hall, you wouldn't mind if I shared your popcorn with you."

"Oh, Mr. Kendal, you're pushing it now."

David stopped. He pulled her toward him.

"I want my answer now."

"What?"

"I can't wait a second longer. Sophia Burkhalter, will you marry me?"

"David, don't you think we should discuss this with Carissa?"

"Sophia, will you marry me?" he repeated.

"What about my career? What about yours?"

"Will you marry me?" His voice became strained.

"David…"

She saw Mary Alice standing only a few feet away, waving as she ran toward them. "Did y'all forget which house?"

A plume of black smoke hung over their yard.

"I sense that Jeremy is grilling." David turned from Sophia and smiled at their friend as she neared them.

"Yeah, he's on the second set of steaks. We've been married long enough I know to buy extras. He'll always burn the first set." She blew a stray hair from her eyes. "I don't know why he insists on grilling them if he's just going to ruin them."

"Maybe I'd better go supervise." David let go of Sophia's hand and headed toward the Krantzes' backyard without another glance in her direction.

"Is everything okay? He seems tense." Mary Alice laced her arm with Sophia's as they walked toward the house.

"He's asked me to marry him." She held out her hand and showed her the ring.

"Sophie!" Mary Alice stopped mid-step and hugged her

friend. "You're getting married?"

"I haven't said yes yet."

"But you're going to, right?"

Sophia just smiled at her dearest friend. "Yes, I think I'm going to marry him."

"I'm so excited for you."

"But don't say anything. I haven't given him an answer yet."

"Why?"

"I want to talk to Carissa. This isn't just between us. This is much bigger than just David and me now. And I need to talk to Pablo, too."

"Why Pablo?"

Sophia shrugged. "I owe him that. He's been the one taking care of me for the past ten years."

"Or keeping you away." She pursed her lips and shook her head. "Well, I get to throw the bridal shower."

"He wants a baby, too." That stopped Mary Alice. "Adopt a baby," Sophia amended.

"And what about you? How do you feel about that?"

"If we got married, I think we could talk about it. But to throw that out there now, I just don't think it was necessary. He raised a daughter. Why would he want to start over now? Just for me?"

"Is that what he told you?"

"Well, no," she confessed as they started up the steps to the house. "I think he feels like he missed out on the early joys of parenting. He started parenting a seven-year-old. He didn't get to hold her or change her diapers or pick her name. She didn't say *daddy* as her first word—at least, not to him."

"She wasn't just a sweet little girl either," Mary Alice recalled.

"What do you mean?"

"She was angry. She hated him, even though she was trying hard to love him. She hated Mandy and still does. That first year, he was at the school almost every day because she was picking fights and not turning in assignments." She shook her head. "God, look at her now. She's an honor student, student council officer, volunteer, and as talented as you are on that cello. He's done a great job."

"See, he just had to do all the work, and he didn't get to enjoy her."

"He enjoys her now. The rest is the past."

"But how do I really know that's what he wants?" Sophia turned to her friend.

"He asked you for it. If he didn't want it, he wouldn't have asked."

"You're right. I know, you're right." She hugged Mary Alice.

"It'll all work out." She opened the front door. "C'mon, I have a great bottle of wine I've been saving just for tonight, and I think you could use a glass."

David grabbed a beer from the cooler on the porch as he walked around the side of the house to where Jeremy stood among the billowing smoke from the grill.

"Damn, I thought you'd have learned how to grill by now." He twisted off the top of the bottle and took a long, needed drink.

"Sooner or later," Jeremy answered as flames kicked up after he flipped a steak. "It's amazing she still lets me try."

"Well, maybe I'll grill the next dinner in my own yard."

"Oh, yeah. Your house will be ready soon."

"I'm putting it up for sale."

"What?"

"I met with a real estate agent today, and she's going to

list the house. It's just too far away. Carissa needs to be closer to school and her friends for her senior year."

He shook his head at his friend's stare.

"Your steaks are on fire." David laughed as Jeremy turned back to the grill.

"Dammit!" He moved the steaks from side to side and rolled cobs of corn into different positions. "You'll stay at Katie's then?"

"I looked at a house."

"Nearby?"

"You could say that. It's over on Cherry Street." He smiled, lifting the beer to his lips as Jeremy realized what he was talking about.

"Your old house?"

"Yep."

"Why?"

"I asked Sophie to marry me."

"Wow! That was fast." He pulled the steaks from the flame and slapped them onto the serving tray.

"Not really. It's been a long time coming. I figure if I keep asking, sooner or later I'll make it all the way to the altar with her. I don't want to waste ten more years."

"Well, you always did have the patience of a saint." He pulled the corn from the grill and closed the lid. "What else is going on? You look lost, my friend. I can see it."

There were many secrets he could hide from Jeremy, and he wasn't sure he wanted to keep it all a secret anymore. It was only going to fester if he didn't talk to someone.

"Mandy's back." He felt the churning in his stomach as he watched Jeremy's face change.

"Shit."

"Tell me about it. Thing is"—he took a breath and dragged his fingers through his hair—"she's pregnant."

Jeremy turned, and his face had gone white. "You didn't."

"No. Not me. Not this time." He waved off any inquisition.

Jeremy nodded, and David took another long pull from his beer.

"She wants me to take the baby."

"She's crazy. But then I've always told you that. Why you?"

"She's dying."

"Sure she is." He snorted.

David let it simmer a moment. "She says that her past drug use has destroyed her heart. I guess having this baby will kill her."

Jeremy's mouth gaped. "What does Sophia say?"

"I haven't told her yet."

"You're thinking about it though. I can see it in your face. Are you nuts?" He was keeping his voice at a whisper, and David appreciated it.

"The baby is Carissa's blood." He shrugged. "It'll be her sister I turn away if I say no." He looked toward Sophia. She and Mary Alice were laughing as they set the table. "Besides, it's Sophia's chance to have a baby."

"Do you really think she'll go for that? It's Mandy's baby."

"I don't know. But I do know she'll stay for Carissa. Why wouldn't she accept this as her opportunity to have a family with me? To have Carissa's sister?" When he said it, it almost seemed logical.

"God, I sure am glad I'm not in your shoes."

CHAPTER ELEVEN

Hand in hand, they left their friends' house and strolled in the warm air of the August night. It was almost eleven o'clock, but the moon was full and lit their way.

David watched Sophia as the moonlight played softly on her hair. If she left him now, he was sure he wouldn't recover this time. He was anxious about everything.

He'd told Sally Foster he wanted the house on Cherry Street, and he wanted the new house put up for sale the moment he closed on it. She'd told him she'd already had two other offers on the house. She'd let him know on the progress, but of course, she'd be happy to list the other.

Sophia caught his glance and smiled.

"You seemed very preoccupied tonight. Are you all right?"

"Yes."

"You're worried about Carissa, aren't you? I mean, you mentioned the house and about her having to drive back here all the time."

"I guess I'm worried about her."

"Tell me about her. Tell me *all* about her."

"What don't you already know?"

Sophia stopped, and David turned to her. "David." She closed her eyes and inhaled. "I was foolish enough to not stick around and ask questions ten years ago. I want to know about her and Mandy. I want to hear it all from you. I'm here now, and I'm asking."

He wiped his brow.

"What do you really want to know?"

"Who was she? Where did you meet her? How did you get involved with her? How…" The expression on her face was open and sincere. But would she feel the same way about him once she knew the truth?

"Okay…okay." David took a deep breath and dove in. "I was twenty-three years old. I was starting my first job with a charter company. Mandy was the daughter of one of the executives that used our company a lot. We met at a holiday party. I think I'd had a few drinks and, well, she was more than a little tipsy." Sophia squeezed his hand, and he continued.

"She seduced me, and I let her. Right there in the hangar, I did something I've never been proud of, but…" he paused. "We saw each other for a few weeks. Hell, we had sex for a few weeks. I guess I'm a big enough man to call it what it was."

He chewed the inside of his cheek. What he was telling Sophia had to be hurting her. He'd never regretted his mistake with Mandy more, yet how could he when she'd given him Carissa?

"I got a new job with the airline. I transferred, and that was the end of it."

"So you left her and didn't see her again until the day you walked out our door?" She'd tied up the story in a neat, little package and pulled him closer. "Doesn't seem like much, does it?"

"Sophie, there's more."

He felt her brace herself against him as they walked.

"She found me in Chicago. That's where I was for about a year before moving back to Kansas City. She was pregnant and thought I should know." Her grip on his hand tightened. "Then she told me she was seventeen."

Sophia stopped. He turned to her. The moonlight shimmered on her tears.

"Sophie, I was stupid. I know that." He lifted her chin and looked her in the eyes. "I never loved her. I never would have...well, had I known how young she was or what kind of person..."

She gasped for breath. It broke his heart to see her cry. He wiped away her tears with his thumb.

"Oh, Sophia, you have to understand..."

"Stop! Stop!" She pushed his hands away and wiped away her tears as fast as they fell. "Carissa was seven when she came to our house."

"Yes."

She set her jaw and her eyes narrowed on him. "God, I wish I would have taken the time to talk to you about this."

"So do I," he confessed and took a step toward her.

Her hand shot up between them and stopped him from touching her. "You knew Mandy was pregnant."

"Yes. She came to me and told me, but said she didn't want anything from me, which was a lie. I wanted to know my child, and she wouldn't let me. She disappeared."

"But you knew."

He let out a breath. "Yes, I knew."

"You son of a bitch." She pounded her fists into his chest. "You never told me!"

"Why? What would it have changed?"

"It was honesty. It's called honesty!"

"Dammit, Sophia. She lied to me."

She jerked away from him and ran down the sidewalk.

"Sophia!" He caught up with her and spun her toward him. "She called and told me Carissa died at birth. I believed her. Do you have any idea how that tore me up? I had no idea that for seven years I'd been a parent."

"God, David, that's not the point." Again, she wiped at her cheeks and looked up at him. "I wanted a baby."

"I know."

"You got someone else pregnant. Don't you think that's a pertinent fact?"

"I got someone pregnant four years before I fell in love with you. No, I didn't see it as pertinent, especially since I couldn't get you pregnant."

Her face crumpled. His careless words had hurt her more than the truth about his fling with Mandy. All he wanted was to take care of her, but he couldn't seem to stop from ripping at her.

She turned and ran again. He ran after her, but she didn't slow.

"Sophia! God, I love you." He finally caught her in the front yard of her grandmother's house. "What in the hell is wrong with you?" He sucked in a breath.

"You should have told me. Dammit, you owed me that much."

"You would have left me."

She only stood there, looking at him.

"Well, I guess had I asked questions instead of running away, things would be clearer now."

"Yes, they would." He held his breath, praying she'd forgive him.

"Instead of considering your proposal, I would have just stayed away forever." She ran through the front door, up the stairs past Carissa, who was sitting in the shadows waiting for them. Sobs shook his daughter's shoulders.

Carissa stood as Sophia ran past her. She would have followed her had her father not burst through the door at the same time calling after her.

"Dammit!" He bent over, bracing his hands on his knees.

"What happened? Why do you always fight with her? Why are you trying to push her away?"

He stood, his mouth gaping in an expression of hurt.

Tears burned her eyes, and she brushed them away as

they began to fall.

"Please, don't mess this up. I want her to stay. This is my first real opportunity to have a mother." She moved in closer to him. "I want that. I deserve that. You can't mess this up for me."

Her dad sat on the step and buried his face in his hands.

Carissa sat down next to him, and he took her hand in his.

"Can't you fix this?"

"Sweetheart, I think this is only the beginning of our troubles."

"I know."

"You do?"

"She came by the shop tonight when I was at work." She looked at him. His eyes searched hers as though they were looking for confirmation. "Mandy."

"I figured." He stood and took her hand. "C'mon, let's make some coffee. This could be a long night."

Carissa sat at the table and watched as her father collected his thoughts while he made coffee. She felt sorry for him. He was being put into positions he'd never asked to be put in, and she was about to make it worse.

"I want you to think about it," she blurted out as he poured the water into the coffeemaker.

"Think about what, Carissa?"

"She told me she wants you to raise the baby."

"Yes, well, it isn't my responsibility. Even considering taking the baby would push Sophia right out of my life, if I haven't already done that."

He pulled down two mugs from the cupboard and set them on the counter.

Carissa chewed her fingernail. It was a nervous habit she'd never been able to control.

"I have a vested interest in this, you know."

"I assumed you'd say something like that." He filled the mugs and carried them to the table. He sat down next to her. "Why do you think I should do this?"

"No matter what she's done, no matter how much I hate her, she's carrying my sister in there."

"Did she tell you the rest of the story?"

"She said she was clean, and she'd had an affair with some married man." He nodded. "Dad, she's going to die."

"Well, at least her stories are holding up. How do you feel about that?"

"I don't give a shit." The obscenity made him snap his head up. "I'm not thinking about Mandy. She's never done anything to warrant my respect or my love. To be honest with you, I think of Sophia more as my mother, and she's only been here a week. But Hope doesn't deserve this."

"Hope?"

"That's what I named the baby. It's what she deserves. A little hope." She curled her hands around the mug in front of her.

"*You* named the baby?" She nodded, her eyes averted. "What did Mandy say to that?"

"I didn't tell her. I really only listened to her." Her eyes shifted back to his. "Really, Dad, all I wanted to do was push her out of the store and lock the door."

He laughed behind his mug.

"Don't you think we need to discuss this with Sophia?"

"Why?"

"I've asked her to marry me."

"So, you're getting married?" Her voice rose with the anticipation of finally having a mother and seeing her father happy.

Her dad cracked a smile, and this time he didn't try to hide it.

"I've asked. She hasn't answered me, and I asked her to wait to do so until she's ready. But if I'm thinking about going along with this, she should be involved, right?"

"Do you think she'll go for it?" Her voice caught. She'd never wanted two things so much in her life. She knew the chance of getting them both was slim.

"Honey, I don't know what to think. Right now my head is spinning."

"Together we can make her consider this." She tried to remain calm as she laid her hand on her father's.

"But what if she doesn't want the baby? What if she doesn't want Mandy's baby?"

The warmth in Carissa's face cooled. Tears pooled in her eyes.

"Dad, she's my sister. I can't just let her go."

David lay in bed and stared at the ceiling.

In his heart, he didn't want to think that Sophia might consider leaving for good, but his head knew better. Add a baby to the mix—correction, add Mandy's baby to the mix—and she was all but gone. But he couldn't break Carissa's heart like that.

He blew out a breath. What in the hell was he going to do?

He rolled to his side and pounded the pillow into place. Sleep evaded him no matter how hard he tried.

He'd come to grips with the fact he'd be a father again to another one of Mandy's daughters. He'd considered not doing it. And with Carissa not being of legal age, she couldn't step in and take the baby either. But he couldn't let her down.

Sophia, he knew, was going to be a bigger challenge. He needed to have everything in place before he could even consider telling her. He'd have to make sure Carissa didn't tell her either.

He'd call Jeremy's brother in the morning. He was a lawyer. They'd need to draw up some paperwork. He'd be damned if he agreed to do this, and she didn't die. He wasn't going to foot her medical bills or take care of her again. This was an all-or-nothing deal, and he needed it legally stated.

Then he'd call Sally Foster. The house on Cherry Street would be perfect for them. But it would be more perfect if Sophia were there with them. If he could secure the house on Cherry Street, maybe she'd consider his proposal again, but still, Sally had said she already had two offers on it.

He looked at the clock. It was four o'clock in the morning. He wanted to go to her room, but he didn't. Instead he fought with himself and tossed in bed until it was time to get up.

Sophia sat by her window looking out at the empty street, the streetlight illuminating her isolation. It was four-thirty in the morning. She'd walked down the hall to David's room. She'd wanted to tap on the door. She had wanted to open it and climb into bed with him. She needed him. Instead, she'd kept quiet and walked back to her own room.

In the morning, she'd make some changes to her life. First of all, she was going to learn to apologize and forgive. Dammit, it was about time. She was going to ask Carissa if she'd be her daughter, and she was going to tell David she'd marry him if Carissa's answer was yes. She was ready for that, too.

Maybe a baby would arrive on their doorstep. Maybe, just maybe, after another call to Sally Foster, the house on Cherry Street would be that very doorstep.

She'd yet to hear from Pablo, and she guessed he'd

have found her at all cost if things had worked out with new venues.

Only one venue had ever escaped them. She often wondered if they'd ever get the chance to perform at the Vatican. Perhaps it was just a dream that would never be reality. However, at that very moment, it didn't matter. She loved David more.

In the morning, well, later in the morning, everything would be okay.

She'd missed him.

"He said he had business and left very early. He dropped Carissa off at work. That's all he said." Katie relayed the information as she poured Sophia a cup of coffee. "Sit down. Let me make you some breakfast."

"I'm not very hungry, Grandma."

"You should eat something."

"I'll get something. Maybe I'll go for a run."

"You're already dressed."

"Yeah, I guess I am." She sat down in the chair at the table.

She'd had all of her words worked out. David would understand. If she said the words *I'm sorry,* he'd forgive her. After all, even after ten years, he'd asked her to marry him.

The doorbell snapped her back to reality. "I'll get that."

She could see the figure beyond the frosted glass of the front door. Without seeing the face, she knew whom it belonged to. An enormous smile crossed her lips, and her heart began to flip in her chest.

"Pablo!" She flung open the door and herself into his arms, which were already out and waiting for her.

"Bella!" He kissed her square on the mouth. Photographic flashes flickered in the street.

"Get in here." With a grimace, she pulled him through

the door and into her arms again. "Where have you been? I've called and called. Oh, Pablo, I've needed you."

She stepped back from him and looked him over. His beauty seemed marred by worry. His dark eyes were heavy, and his wavy, black hair was longer than he usually wore it. His perfect physique was hiding behind a sweatshirt and a snug pair of jeans. The world was used to seeing him looking exquisite. Even Sophia rarely saw him in such relaxed attire.

"Bella, what has you so upset?" He touched her face with the gentleness of a lover.

"Where do I start? But first, what's going on with you? Why haven't you returned my calls?"

Slumping, he let her lead him to the couch where they sat with their fingers interlaced. "Sandra left."

"Why?"

"Sophia, someone has put her up to something. Paid her off for a story about how evil I am."

"That's not true." Her voice rose with her anger.

"Ah, from your lips to God's ears!" He raised his hands. "But it is what it is."

"And Pierre?"

"Oh, Sophia." He gathered her hands in his again. "I know you've kept our secret out of respect for our art and our friendship. Perhaps I even used you a bit in front of the media, which has been pointed out to me." His brows rose, and he shook his head. "But I've never asked you to lie, have I?"

"Goodness, no."

"Well, no longer is there need for you to hold your tongue. Pierre and I are to be married at Christmas."

"Pablo!" She wrapped her arms around his neck and kissed him on the cheek. "I'm so happy for the two of you."

"Thank you. You'll be there?" His heavy Italian accent sang in her ears.

"I wouldn't miss it for the world."

"Good. Then we have one more order of business." He stood and pulled a letter from his pocket and handed it to her.

Sophia opened the letter, and her eyes grew wide. "Oh, Pablo!"

"It's the invitation that we've waited our whole lives for."

"The Vatican."

"The Vatican. Can you believe it, Bella?" His voice was pure and full of joy.

She turned to him, the significance of what he'd said to her about Pierre sinking in. "They don't know about the two of you?"

"Not yet. That's why it is crucial we live out this one, last dream before things that shouldn't matter do."

Sophia nodded. How could loving someone ever be bad? But if the Vatican knew that Pablo DiAngelo intended to marry another man, they'd cancel the performance. Sophia looked at the letter once more.

"Pablo, this is in three days."

"We leave now." The statement was precise.

"But the party."

"You'll give your condolences."

"Oh, Pablo, so much has happened. I have to tell you..."

"Bella, either we go now or we miss out on what we've always wanted. Won't what you want to tell me wait?"

She was sure it would. Her head was spinning when her grandmother entered the room.

"Oh, Grandma." She smiled, crossing the room toward her. "Oh, the most wonderful thing has happened." She noticed her grandmother's eyes shift to the man behind her. "Grandma, you remember Pablo."

"Mrs. Burkhalter, it's a pleasure." Pablo held his hand out while Katie looked him over with skeptical eyes.

"Mr. DiAngelo, how unexpected."

"I know. My apologies."

"Grandma, we've been invited to the Vatican!" Her voice still bubbled over with the enthusiasm of having one of her dreams come true.

"Oh, Sophie, that is wonderful." Her grandmother gathered her in her arms and hugged her tightly.

"It is, isn't it?"

"When?"

Sophia stepped back, and tears began to fill her eyes. "I have to leave now."

"Now?" Disappointment filled her grandmother's voice, and that alone was enough to break Sophia's heart.

"I know. The timing isn't great, but Grandma…"

Katie touched her granddaughter's arm. "I'll have another birthday. If you must, go."

"Oh, thank you." She hugged her grandmother again. "I have to call David. I have to tell him. I have to say goodbye."

"David?" Pablo stepped up to her. "Please, David?"

"Oh, Pablo, that's what I'm trying to tell you. He's asked me to marry him."

His eyes narrowed, and Sophia could see his disappointment. She knew he'd understand when she explained. They'd spent years sharing their stories. Love found. Love lost. He wouldn't look at her like that for long, or so she hoped.

"Go pack. We must leave within the hour."

David sat in the office of Todd Krantz, tapping his

fingers on the desk as Todd read over the contract they had penned.

"I think it's solid," Todd said, sliding it into a folder.

David ran his hands over his face. "God, what am I doing?"

"Well, like you said, you're not obligated to do this. This is not your child."

"I know." His heart was racing. "I know."

"Well, let's get this thing signed." He stood behind his desk and gathered the folder and the paper that bore Mandy's address. They headed out to the car and drove through town toward the motel.

When they pulled up, she peeked through the curtains of the dingy motel window. Sweat had formed on his brow, and his heart was thumping at a particularly unpleasant pace. He took his cell phone out of his pocket and laid it on the seat. The last thing he needed now was an interruption. How would he explain what it was he was doing, especially to Carissa or Sophia?

When Mandy opened the door for them, one look at her told him he was doing the right thing. It had only been a day since he'd seen her, but she looked weaker—as though she had begun dying.

"David, what can I do for you?" Her voice shook, and she swayed.

"Mandy, why don't you sit?" He was already walking through the door before she could slam it in his face.

She didn't argue. David was already nervous, but when she ran the heel of her hand between her breasts to ease the obvious pain she was in, he felt the blood rush from his head, and he too sat down.

"This is Todd Krantz. He's my lawyer."

"Lawyer? Are you suing me?" Her voice dropped to a whisper. David shook his head, and she sighed. "What then?"

"Mandy, I've decided I want to help you. I want your baby." The words sounded like those from a character on one of his aunt's soap operas.

"David, get out." She stood quickly and then sat back down, panting and clutching the arm of the sofa with one hand and her forehead with the other.

"Carissa doesn't want her sister going to strangers. So, if you need to think of this on other terms, think of Carissa."

Her eyes softened. "Carissa. I was sure she thought I was crazy. She didn't say a word to me when I spoke to her."

"Well, she had plenty to say when she got home, but she doesn't want her sister to live with strangers."

"I don't want her to either," Mandy admitted. "But why the lawyer?" She shot a look in Todd's direction.

"I intend to take only the baby. I don't intend to take the mother in this deal." His words were crisp and steered toward hateful. He knew she didn't need further explanation.

"I guess I was a handful last time, wasn't I?"

"I'm not pointing fingers and passing blame. I have Carissa, and that's all I ever wanted from you. Now Carissa wants Hope, and I want her to have her in her life."

"Hope?"

Damn. He hadn't meant to let that slip.

"Hope is what she's named the baby."

"Hope." The name settled on her lips. "I really like that."

Tears were already forming in her eyes. Looking at her, David couldn't remember the young woman who had seduced him in the hangar so many years ago. The eyes he was staring into belonged to someone else—someone who had aged well beyond her years and obviously regretted every moment of it.

"I need to know, honestly, how likely are you to survive this?"

"The contractions will most likely set off my heart's rhythm. Even if they give me medication in the hospital, my heart is that weak. They can do a transplant, but I don't want that." She moved closer to him and covered his hand with hers. It felt cool and skeletal. "I'm okay with this, especially now." She smiled, but he couldn't muster one. "Since you're here and so is he"—she nodded in Todd's direction—"I want you to know that I don't want them to resuscitate me. I want to die."

Her words slammed into him. He hadn't expected them to. He hadn't expected to care, but his heart wouldn't let her suffer before and it wouldn't now.

Todd stepped in. "Mandy, I admire your courage. David wants what's best for both of your girls. We've drawn up some papers that say you give up all parental rights to the baby and give them to David."

"Give them to me. I'll sign them."

"They also state that if you survive the birth there are no obligations owed to you by Mr. Kendal and you will not seek custody of your daughter or reimbursement for medical expenses."

"I said I'd sign them." She reached her hand out.

David wanted to speak. He wanted to apologize. He wanted to tell her not to sign the papers, but he couldn't.

He watched her sign away her daughter and essentially her life.

"Keep the name," she said on a weak breath.

"What?"

"Hope. I want that to be her name."

"Okay." He drew in a deep breath. "How does this all

go down?"

Mandy winced and rubbed her stomach. "I have DNR papers, medical papers, and my will in my purse. You need to be there with me when I go into labor and have the baby. My will already states you as the baby's father, but I want your name on the birth certificate."

"I'll be there. Where can I write down my cell phone number?"

Todd handed him the note pad by the phone. He jotted down the number and his schedule for the following week and handed it to her.

"Tell me if you think you'll go longer. I'll cancel my work schedule, too."

"I'm sure it'll be soon. I've been having a lot of contractions." She winced and rubbed her stomach again.

"Maybe you shouldn't be alone."

"I'll be fine."

David nodded and stood to leave.

"David," she called after him. "Thank you. This means so much to me."

He couldn't answer. He only nodded as he and Todd left the motel.

He picked up his cell phone from the seat as he sat down. It rang in his hand, but he let it continue to ring. It was Sophia.

He silenced it and slid it into his pocket. His voice wouldn't be steady. Not yet. He couldn't come up with the words to tell her what he'd just done for his daughter. He wasn't sure Sophia loved him enough to accept it.

He blew out a breath and rubbed his chest with his palm, easing away the ache much as Mandy had done earlier.

CHAPTER TWELVE

Sophia threw items from the bathroom counter into the half-packed suitcase on her bed. A flicker of movement nearby made her jump.

"Oh, Grandma! You scared me to death." She threw the items in her hands into the suitcase and returned to the closet.

"When are you leaving?"

"As soon as I get downstairs." She shook her head. "I can't believe he finally got the Vatican. Oh, Grandma, this is so amazing!"

"Yes, it sure is. What did David say?"

"I keep calling his phone, but he won't answer. Carissa doesn't answer either."

"What about Carissa's audition?" Katie folded a shirt that Sophia had tossed on the bed and set it into the suitcase for her.

Sophia paused, her hands full of expensive clothes she'd purchased in Europe. "Do you think she'll hate me?"

"She is seventeen."

Sophia knew her grandmother well enough that she understood her grandmother didn't want her to go, but would never stop her either.

"I'll be back."

"When?" Katie shot back.

"I don't know."

"What about David? You're going to marry him, aren't you?"

"We have a lot to work out. He's done some things..."

"And you're walking away again," Katie reminded her.

"For something I've always wanted." She dropped a

dress into her suitcase.

"What if he changes his mind?"

"Maybe I've already changed mine." She shut the suitcase and zipped it closed.

"You've had *another* fight?"

"Yes, yes we did." The answer was as matter-of-fact as it could be. "There are just some things we can't see eye to eye on."

"I see."

Sophia stopped and took a deep breath. She turned to Katie and took her hands. "I love you, Grandma. I'm coming back. I promise. Whether I become Mrs. David Kendal or not, I'll be here. I already have my things in Seattle being shipped to me. I've looked at a house, and who knows, maybe someday I'll teach music." The thought appealed to her more than ever. "I want to be here to see Carissa become an adult, even if she doesn't become my daughter. My life is here."

"But, for now, you have to go?"

"Yes."

Katie nodded. "What do I tell David and Carissa?"

"That I'll be back very soon." She saw the trepidation on her grandmother's face. She'd run away from her fears once, and she wouldn't do it again. "And this time I promise."

As David and Carissa walked through the door, Katie set the last serving dish on the table.

David surveyed the room. He looked at the table and noted the four plates.

Carissa set her purse on the counter and hugged Millie.

"Oh, this looks good. I'm so hungry."

"Good." Millie's voice broke.

"Where is she?" His voice was already shaky.

"Gone," Katie said as she sat down to the table.

"Gone? Gone where?" He hadn't taken another step into the room.

"David, sit," Millie instructed, and his eyes darted to hers. "Sit."

The pain in his chest was back. She hadn't gotten over their fight. Damn! She was the most stubborn, most pigheaded, most...

"Pablo came for her today." Katie sat with her hands in her lap and her head lowered to pray.

Carissa's eyes darted to his, and he tightened his jaw.

Again, Millie instructed, "Sit!"

David sat. He bowed his head. He listened to the prayer, and then he shot back up to his feet.

"I can't believe this!"

"Dad, calm down." Carissa shot up next to him. "Maybe there's a good explanation."

"No." He turned to Millie and Katie. "What happened?"

"They got their invitation to the Vatican." Katie's voice was soft, but there was an edge to it. David caught it.

"You just let her go?"

"Don't be disrespectful, Davie," Millie intervened, as if he was a child.

"I didn't have a choice." Katie began to serve herself dinner. "This is what she wanted. It's what she's always wanted. She said she'd be back soon."

David raked his fingers through his hair and spun on his heels. He needed air. He pulled his phone out of his pocket. She'd called him six times while he was in Todd's office and with Mandy.

Shit! She'd tried to call him and tell him, and he wasn't there. What he'd been doing now felt deceitful, and his insides twisted until he was sick.

Carissa followed him to the back porch.

"It would have been nice. Wouldn't it have?" She sat on the steps to the porch, pulled her long, dark hair over her shoulder, and wrapped it around her fingers. "I thought she'd stay. I thought she'd be my mother."

Tears welled in her eyes. David wrapped his arm around her shoulders and kissed her on the top of the head, blinking back the moisture in his own eyes.

"We're making assumptions." He tried to remain optimistic. "We haven't talked to her. So, she's not here. She'll miss the party." That alone had a bad taste in his mouth. Katie deserved more than what Sophia had offered.

"She'll miss my audition," Carissa added, and that set David's teeth to grinding. Another promise broken.

"But she helped you. Do your best, and get that seat." It wasn't a suggestion. It was a demand, and she nodded. "She'll call. Even if she's mad at me, she'll call you." He was sure of it.

"Do you think she'll come back?" She looked up at him, tears streaking her cheeks.

He wiped his thumb over her tears and rested his head against his daughter's. His entire body ached with missing Sophia. "I don't know."

By the time she returned, he'd be a father again. He couldn't even begin to convince his daughter Sophia would stay.

During the first three hours on the plane, Sophia drank four cups of coffee, excused herself to the bathroom six times, and broke down in tears more than once. She was a wreck.

"My Bella, I thought you'd be happy to come home with me." Pablo took her hand in his and interlaced their fingers, stopping her from wringing his prized possessions.

He gently lifted her hand to his lips and kissed each finger. "Why are you so sad?"

"I love him, Pablo. Dear God, I love him. I shouldn't have left." Tears welled in her eyes, but she fought them back.

"I thought you were over him. I thought you'd moved on in your life." His voice resonated with anger, and she couldn't blame him.

"I thought I had, but I was wrong." She turned in her seat to look him in the eye. "Oh, Pablo! He still loves me. I was so wrong about everything, and I ran away without asking questions or trying to find out what was what. I was a fool. I love him."

"I can have them turn the plane around if you'd like." His eyes softened, and he even smiled.

"Oh, shut up." She laughed a weak laugh and laid her head on his shoulder. "I love you."

"And I love you, Bella." He rested his head to hers and she closed her eyes, hoping she hadn't sacrificed the people she loved most to play at the Vatican.

David paced the floor through the night and into the morning. Sophia hadn't even called. He was furious.

He held the box that the glassblower had given him in his hand. He hadn't had an opportunity to give her the gift he'd brought back from Hawaii. On his dresser now lay the picture of her and her parents that he'd taken from her apartment. He thought she should have it with her.

No matter what time her flight had been, she'd surely have landed in Rome by now and should have called. He'd had enough waiting. Dammit, he'd call her.

He opened his cell phone. The digital clock on the phone read 3:00 a.m. He hit her name on his speed dial. He heard it ring. He heard it again. Then he heard a tap on his door.

Quickly, he flung it open with hopes that somehow she'd be there.

Carissa stood in the doorway in her pajamas. Her eyes were red and swollen. In her hand was Sophia's phone.

"It was on her bed." She clutched the phone to her chest. "Do you think she'll come back?"

He gathered his daughter in his arms and held her tight. He didn't have an answer for her this time.

Sophia had meant to call home, but there had been no time. The moment they'd stepped off the plane, the paparazzi were there. She'd never get used to the press as Pablo had.

He wrapped his arm protectively around her, and Pierre walked a few steps behind them. She'd been Pablo's front for so many years, but she'd never realized it until they walked through the airport in Rome. She thought of all the pictures her grandmother had hanging in the hallway of her house. It was no wonder David had assumed Pablo was her lover.

Pablo had them driven straight to his rehearsal hall, and they began putting together their program. He threw out songs to them, they played, and he sang.

"Bella! What have you been doing?" he screamed. "You're flat!

"I most certainly am not." She was edgy from lack of sleep and disappointment from not telling David goodbye. Pablo hadn't even given her the time to call him again.

"Get it right."

"Bite me," she huffed out under her breath, but he heard it.

"Oh, Americans!"

"Oh, stubborn Italians!"

The sliver of a smile creased his lips, and Thomas stifled a laugh at the piano.

"She's home!" He tapped his hand on his heart. "She's home."

"Pablo, let's break for dinner." Pierre laid his hand on Pablo's shoulder, kneading it gently. "We've all been up too long, and rehearsal is going nowhere."

Pablo took his hand in his and kissed it.

"Okay, my love. Dinner."

They packed up their belongings and, again, huddled together as camera flashes pursued them to their car.

"I hate them all!" Pablo let go of Sophia's hand and grasped Pierre's in his own just as soon as they left the rest of the world outside the limousine. "Since the moment that *woman* left our ensemble, they have been like vultures. They will rue the day they came up against Pablo DiAngelo."

Pierre wiped a lock of hair from Pablo's forehead. "Soon, my love. Soon it will all be over, and we will have nothing to hide. And they can take all the pictures they want at our ceremony."

Pablo kissed Pierre's fingers.

"Speaking of weddings." Pablo lifted Sophia's hand and raised an eyebrow. "This?"

"Yes, this." She tilted her hand to examine the ring that had adorned her finger a decade earlier. Thomas shifted uncomfortably in his seat, and Pierre shook his head and patted her knee.

"Oh, Sophia, why did you come?"

"Pablo asked me to."

"He's mine, not yours. I'll take care of him."

"Oh, I meant no disrespect." She bit her lip and turned her body toward Pierre.

"I know, but he's pigheaded!" Pierre held his hand up in defense to stop Pablo from speaking. "He thinks he needs your image to guide him through this life. But he's wrong. I love him, and that should be enough."

Sophia suddenly realized the conversation wasn't for her. It was for Pablo, who took Pierre's face in his hands and kissed him full on the mouth.

When they pulled apart, he murmured, "*Ti amo.*"

"Then act like it. When we step out of this car, hold my hand, not hers."

"I can't do that." He dropped his head.

"You're a coward!" Pierre crossed his arms over his chest and one leg over the other, bouncing his foot in defiance.

"Yes, I am. But as we leave the Vatican, I will hold your hand."

"I quit," Sophia piped up, and all the men stared at her.

Pablo turned to face her. "I beg your pardon."

"I mean when it's all over, I quit." Saying the words filled her with optimism.

"Now, Sophia, just because I'm fighting with him doesn't…"

She shook her head. Everything seemed clearer now. Brighter.

"No, no. It's not that. I just realized that I love David more than this now. I want to marry him and have children with him. Carissa!"

"Carissa?" Pierre snorted a laugh. "What's a Carissa?"

"She'll be my daughter!" She was giddy inside. Her stomach fluttered, and her heart raced wildly. "Oh, I'll be a mother! And he wants to adopt more children!" Her voice had laughter in it, and Pierre smiled even though Pablo was frowning. Thomas had turned his head and stared out into the lights of Rome. She reached for her purse. "I have to call them."

Sophia searched through her things. She couldn't find

her cell phone in its usual compartment and began tossing items from her purse onto the floor. But her phone wasn't there.

"Damn!"

"Bella, we will be done in a few days. Enough of this silliness." Pablo crossed his arms over his massive chest and looked straight ahead.

She knew he was right. David wasn't going anywhere. He'd be home when she got there. It might be rough for a few days, but he'd accept her apology. But damn! She wanted to talk to Sally Foster. She'd told her she had a good chance at the house. She hadn't thought about leaving town and losing it all together. She had to get to a phone.

Thomas handed her his phone just as the car came to a stop.

"Thank you." She smiled at the young pianist, who warmly returned the gesture.

She began to dial as she was pulled from the car. Chaos ensued, and she was forced to slip the phone into her purse and forgo the call. There were photographers and people everywhere, all waiting to get a peek at Sophia and Pablo. Pierre and Thomas were their regular two steps behind them when Pablo waved to his admirers and took her hand in his. Sophia lowered her head to get through the crowd.

She'd always hated living the public life, and Pablo had always embraced it. A reporter yelled from the crowd.

"Sophia! What's the scar on your neck from?"

Instinctively her hand shot up to her bare neck. No one had ever seen her without her trademark scarves or pearls. Warrior! Warrior! Damn! She wanted to cry. Then another question flew from the crowd.

"Beautiful ring! Are you two getting married soon?"

God! They thought Pablo was really her fiancé.

Another yelled out, "Pablo, what about your affair with

Pierre?"

Pierre's face flushed red, and he lunged after the reporter.

Sophia couldn't tell who hit whom first, but a moment later, she was on the ground next to Pablo, armed guards surrounding them.

Pierre lay unconscious, blood trickling from his mouth.

Carissa was filling the house with a Pablo DiAngelo song, and David could smash the cello into a million pieces, the way he was feeling.

He'd just picked up this morning's newspaper when his cell phone rang. He flipped it open. He'd given up on it being Sophia.

"Mr. Kendal, I'm with the title company. We need to set up a time for your closing on Thursday."

Right. David had to move on with his life.

He scheduled the closing.

His coffee had gone cold. As he opened the paper, everything went bitter.

The entertainment section of the paper sprawled over the table. Photos of Sophia and Pablo, hand in hand, made his chest tighten. Their fingers were interlocked. The story went on about a rock on her hand and a wedding in their future. Someone had even caught them on the plane sleeping. Her head rested on his shoulder and his on her head, and a blanket covered them both. Very intimate.

He'd been such a fool. He crumpled the paper into a ball and threw it in the trash. Within the week, he and Carissa would be taking Hope to their new home and starting a chapter of his life he'd never anticipated. And it was obvious he'd be doing that without Sophia.

Mandy called later in the afternoon, and David felt his

stomach flop.

"I'd like a ride to the doctor."

"Are you okay?" Panic vibrated through his voice.

"I'm fine. Seems I can't get behind the wheel of that old car anymore." She laughed. "I thought maybe Carissa could take me."

"She moved her audition. She's there now. I'll come get you."

Within the hour, he was driving Mandy to her doctor's appointment. His palms were sweating, and his heart was racing. He should have been doing these things when she was pregnant with Carissa.

"Why do you have a doctor appointment in town?"

"I've never been far away from you guys. Not physically, that is."

"You've been in Kansas City the whole time?" His eyes darted from the road to her.

"Yes."

He almost said, *It would have been nice if you'd come by to see your daughter,* but it wouldn't have been true. He shook his head. The woman would never cease to amaze him.

He helped her out of the car, and she checked in at the desk. She was escorted back to the exam room within a few moments of arrival.

David made himself comfortable in the waiting area. The receptionist puttered around the room, tidying up the kids' toys in the bucket and the magazines on the tables.

"Oh, he's a sexy one." She smiled as she laid the magazine on the table beside him. "Wouldn't mind him burning my eggs in the morning."

David couldn't help but look at what seemed to be a perfectly mannered woman. What would make her say such a thing? He looked down at the magazine she'd laid by him, and, as big as life, there was Pablo in his black tuxedo, mouth open, no doubt an amazing sound escaping it.

Curiosity had caught him. He opened the magazine, which was dated a week earlier.

The article was all about Pablo DiAngelo and his lover, Pierre Van Volden. He tucked his lips between his teeth and read. Caught with the flutist in an intimate situation, he'd denied the rumors. The article went on to talk about the quick dismissal of Sandra Valdez and the absence of Sophia Burkhalter.

David shook his head. He certainly had never cared for Pablo DiAngelo. The man had given Sophia a life she otherwise would never have had, but he was deceiving the world, too. Sophia would figure that out eventually. He was just afraid it was going to be too late.

His attention snapped back to the matter at hand when a nurse entered the waiting room.

"Your wife would like to see you." He stared at her blankly as she spoke. "Mr. Kendal?"

"Yes."

"Mrs. Kendal would like you to come back and see the pictures of the baby."

Mrs. Kendal? There had to be a mistake, and he'd put an end to that!

The nurse opened the door and Mandy lay on the table, her enlarged stomach exposed. The doctor in his white coat slathered her stomach with a gel and rubbed a wand over her skin.

"Mr. Kendal, you're just in time."

Mandy held her hand out to him, and he took it. The image came up on the screen, and his heart was gone.

"Isn't she beautiful?" Mandy asked. David could only nod.

"Is she okay?" He directed his question to the doctor.

"She looks really good. Your wife is dilated at a three.

You should see this little one in a day or so."

David's eyes and heart were lost to the image on the screen. Would she look like Carissa? Would her hair be black as coal like hers? Would she have her brown, puppy-dog eyes?

"Okay, Mrs. Kendal, go ahead and get dressed. I'm going to speak to your husband in my office." The doctor patted her knee.

David followed the doctor to his office and sat down in the chair opposite the doctor, who laid Mandy's file on his desk.

"I'm glad to finally meet you. This has been a long road for your wife. She's been very strong about it all, but I know she's scared."

David hated Mandy for making him take part in this charade. But in order for him to get custody of the baby, they had to think he was her father.

"She's made up her mind. She knows what she wants."

"I think we can sustain her life, at least for a little while, and we can get her on a donor's list. It wouldn't be pleasant for her."

"And she's agreed to this?" David moved to the edge of his chair. His jaw clenched.

"No. She's sure that when the time comes, she wants to go."

David couldn't decide if the settling of his stomach was relief or understanding. He wouldn't want to be kept alive, but still be dying, either.

"I'll go with her wishes."

The doctor nodded. "She said the two of you have a seventeen-year-old daughter."

"Yes." Even though that was the truth, he didn't like the way it sounded.

"Well, I'm sure she'll be a big help to you. But Mr.

Kendal, please consider helping her change her mind. She'd want to see the baby."

David said he'd discuss it with Mandy, and he left the office and returned to the reception area. Mandy joined him a moment later, looking paler and more fragile. She took his hand and steadied herself. He had to wrap an arm around her shoulders to help her to the car.

He lowered her to her seat and walked around to the other side. He slid behind the wheel and took a deep breath. "Why am I'm listed as your husband?"

She turned toward him and spoke softly, "I thought it would be easier."

"You've had me down as your husband since the beginning, haven't you?" She nodded with her eyes averted. "You knew I'd take this baby?"

"I'm sorry. I didn't see the harm. I figured if you took her, they couldn't question me. If you didn't, no one would know any better."

"Show me your driver's license."

"What?"

"Show me!" He watched her as she pulled it from her wallet. "Mandy Kendal. How did you pull that off?"

"I just changed my name. I thought..."

"I don't want to hear it." He gripped the steering wheel. "You're right. It will make it easier."

When they reached the motel, he helped her out of the car and noticed she was gasping for breath. "Will you be okay?"

"I'll be fine. I'll call 911 if I need something." She stumbled past him to her door.

"Why are you staying in a motel?"

She unlocked the door to her room and pushed it open.

"I sold everything off so there wouldn't be anything left when I died. The papers in my purse explain it all. I even have my burial expenses paid for, so all you'll have to do is sign me over, and they'll take care of the rest. Nice and tidy, don't you think?"

"Yeah, nice and tidy." Hope would be his child—and her mother was staying in a fleabag motel. It wasn't right. He moved toward her. "You know, you could stay with..."

"No. I know you're wary and think I'm going to do something at the last minute and mess up your life. If you didn't, you wouldn't have drawn up papers." She laid her hand on his chest. "I've changed. I've lived a life of lies, and I've paid for them. My children, however, never deserved to have to pay for my mistakes. You've seen to Carissa, and she turned into a wonderful woman. I could never have given her the life you have. I want Hope to have that same chance. Give that to her, David."

"I will," he promised.

Mandy took a shallow breath. "Sophia will be a wonderful mother."

The words punched David in the gut.

"We'll see."

He helped her into her room and got her situated. "I'll be around if you need me. Tomorrow I have a meeting. So if you need anything..."

"I'll be fine." She held out her hand to him. "David, thank you again."

He only nodded and left her.

She was right. He was leery as hell over her change of heart. He'd never been too convinced that someone as messed up as Mandy could have changed. But he was witnessing firsthand a complete turnaround. In fact, he was beginning to feel sorry for her. Shaking the thought from his head, he drove away. He'd felt sorry for her last time, and it had cost him the woman he loved. He winced at the thought. It just might have done it again.

CHAPTER THIRTEEN

Carissa watched her dad hang up the phone as she blew on her fingernails. The color of the polish only irritated her now. She should change it, just for spite.

"What did Ms. Foster say?"

"The house on Cherry Street sold already." He ran his fingers through his hair. "I guess we should just keep ours and decide what to do."

"Dad, I can go to school out by the new house. I know it's too hard to commute. Besides, I can be there to take care of Hope."

"It's not fair to ask you to do that. You'd have to give up your job and first chair. You earned that chair. You worked hard for that. Sophia would be proud."

"She will be proud." She put a positive twist on the words she spoke, which his were lacking. "Don't give up on her, Dad. Pablo's not in love with her. He's in love with the flutist. I don't think she's ever thought of Pablo that way."

Her father cringed and let out a sigh.

"She might come home to us, honey, but it won't be just us, will it?"

Carissa shook her head. "Hope."

"Yeah, Hope." He fidgeted with his phone.

"Dad, if you want to back out…"

"No." He shot his head up to look at her. "She's mine." A smile slid across his lips when he said it.

"You are the most amazing man. I know Sophia will see that."

"You're too kind." He stood and kissed her on the cheek. "We'll see what happens. Let's see if she even comes home. But first I think we'd better go do some shopping."

"Shopping? Dad, are you okay?"

"Mandy is going to have that baby any minute. We'd better have a crib, some diapers, and some clothes for her."

"Oh, yeah. Wow, Dad." Her own baby sister. She hugged herself, and then she hugged him. "I can't believe we're going to be three of us."

He squeezed her hard. After a second, he turned away and wiped his hands under his eyes. "Neither can I."

Within three hours, they had purchased everything they needed for the baby. They drove it out to the new house they'd had built. What was to be the spare room had to be transformed into a nursery.

"I hope she likes princesses." Carissa deposited another armful of little outfits onto the stack of Hope's bedding and clothing.

"Honey, you like them. She'll love them." He patted her knee from where he knelt on the floor, assembling a swing. "Little sisters think the world of big sisters."

"Lots of pressure."

"Yeah, so you'd better walk the straight and narrow. She'll be watching."

"I realize that now." Would she be a good big sister? She hoped so. Carissa sat back on her heels. "Did you tell the ladies?"

"No. Only Todd and Jeremy know. It'll be easier to explain when we have Hope and Mandy is…" He didn't come out and say it, but Carissa was having the same thought.

"I guess we should think about moving things in here this weekend, huh?" The house looked so empty and bare. It needed to be filled…with people who loved it, and loved each other.

"I guess so. You know, maybe we should store the

bassinet in the car and stay with the ladies for the first few days. I just realized I have no idea how to take care of a newborn baby."

A laugh escaped Carissa. "Yeah, a seven-year-old was hard enough for you."

"I did okay."

"Yeah, you did. But c'mon, you have to admit it was a struggle."

"I'll admit it only because you want me to." Her dad was such a goof, and that's exactly the way she loved him.

"I think I turned out okay. It's been years since the principal has called you or since I was in a fight."

"You turned out perfect."

"I did, didn't I?" She touched his arm. "Thanks to you. And Hope will turn out perfect, too."

Sophia boarded the plane in Pennsylvania and blew out a breath when she realized it would be the last leg of her trip. She'd made one phone call to Sally Foster from the airport. She was disappointed to find out that the house had sold. She'd find something in the future. For the time being, she'd live with her grandmother. She'd always be welcome in her grandmother's home.

She looked at her watch. She'd land at two o'clock. The party would end at four. She would at least make it in enough time to make an appearance.

When she was in flight, she took out her mirror, fixed up her makeup, and did what she could with her hair. She'd tried to sleep on the previous flights, but still her eyes looked hollow. She'd worn a sundress, and the gauze material looked like it'd held up to the travel. Instinctively, she tapped her fingers to her Saint Nicholas medal.

Several hours later, she stood outside the church where her Katie and Millie—and David and Carissa—were celebrating the ladies' eighty-fourth birthday. She gulped in a deep breath. Her heart hammered in her chest as she stepped inside.

The room was still full, and laughter surrounded her. Carissa had decorated with the few items they'd purchased together. Katie was leaning over in animated conversation, and she patted her tiara. The table of food was almost completely empty—they'd obviously made good choices.

Mary Alice noticed her and raced across the room. Sophia set down her bags and her instrument a moment before her friend enveloped her in a hug.

"God, I'm glad you're home." She stepped back and looked her over, her hands secured to Sophia's shoulders as if to hold her in place. "You look good."

"Thank you."

"She's right," David said behind her friend. "You look good."

Mary Alice gave her a wink and rejoined the party.

Sophia stood still as David walked around her. His eyes were cold, and she certainly didn't blame him.

"I'm glad you could make it for the party." His voice was shaky. She knew he wanted to be angry, and that he hadn't expected her to return.

"So am I."

"I'm sorry to hear about the Vatican."

"It wasn't meant to be." Her heart ached at all the pain she'd caused him over a dream that never could have come true. She felt like she needed to take the opportunity to apologize right there.

"David, I want to..." Carissa's moving to her father's side interrupted her thought. "Carissa." Her voice thickened as she looked at the girl who had changed so much in the short time she'd known her.

"I told them all that you'd come back. I told them you

didn't leave us for good." Carissa wrapped her arms around Sophia and hugged her tight.

"Sophia." Her grandmother called her, and with a regretful glance at David, she crossed the room to her.

"Happy birthday, Grandma." She kissed her cheek. "Happy birthday, Millie." She moved to kiss David's aunt, who sat in her chair looking weak, Sophia thought. "Your tiaras look wonderful."

"That was a wonderful surprise. Carissa told us how you picked them out for us."

"Yes, we did," she said, realizing Carissa was by her side. She wrapped her arm around her shoulders and leaned her head against hers. She had missed so many years. They both had.

She felt David's presence behind her, and when she felt his hand on her shoulder, she knew she'd been forgiven. She reached her hand to his, and he gave her a squeeze.

"I wanted to apologize to you all for the way I acted. It wasn't until I was in Rome that I realized I wanted you all more than my career or even the Vatican. By then it was too late, and I was stuck there." She turned to David. "I hope you'll forgive me—again."

"Sophie, I love you." He smiled as he caressed her cheek

"I love you." She turned to Carissa. "And I love you."

"Oh, Sophia." Carissa wiped the tears from her cheeks.

"So, let me do this right." She reached to the back of her neck and unclasped the chain that held her Saint Nicholas medal.

"Carissa, when I was little, my mother put this on me. She said it was to protect children. I had it on during our accident," she said, dangling it in her hand. "I guess it worked. I've waited my whole life to pass it on. But I always knew I would only pass it to my child." She took a deep breath as Carissa's eyes widened. "Carissa, would you do me the honor of allowing me to adopt you before you turn eighteen and be your mother?"

Silence had fallen over the hall. Someone sobbed softly.

Carissa stood silent, her mouth gaping. She looked over to her father, who smiled.

She nodded through joyful tears.

"Good, turn around," Sophia instructed, and Carissa turned her back to Sophia and lifted her hair.

Sophia clasped the chain around her neck.

Carissa turned around, grasping it in her fingers, and looked down at it.

"Oh my God." She drew Sophia into her arms for a long hug. "You were already my mom anyway."

It was a long time before Sophia could speak.

"David." She turned to him and looked up into his dark eyes. "We always planned a life together. I never meant for it to fall apart. So now that I have your daughter's approval and she accepts me as her mother, I'd like to ask you, would you do me the honor..."

He was shaking his head. "Stop. Please stop." He took her hands in his. "Sophie, we have a lot of talking to do."

"I know."

"Things have changed around here, and you have no idea. No one does. Our lives are about to change." He exchanged an uneasy glance with Carissa.

"Yes, they are." She was smiling, but he was still shaking his head.

"Do you trust me?"

"Of course I do."

"Do you love me?"

"Oh, David, you know…"

"Do you love me?"

"Yes."

"Will you trust me with your life and the life of your family?"

"Yes."

"And if I made a decision, you'd stand behind me?"

"Yes." Her answer was soft. An icy knot formed in her stomach. "David, what's going on?"

"I want my answer first. I asked you to wait, and now I'm ready. Sophia Burkhalter, will you marry me?"

She smiled. Her heart was racing. Sophia took a breath to give him her answer, but someone screamed his name. Chaos erupted.

An extremely pregnant woman stood in the doorway, clutching her stomach. Her face was ghostly white, and her body swayed. She fell to her knees and then crumpled to the floor.

"Mandy!" David yelled. He raced to the pregnant woman. To Mandy.

"Mom!" Carissa tore away from Sophia and followed him.

Todd and Jeremy Krantz were already at her, assessing her. They started CPR on her.

Sophia backed toward her grandmother. *Carissa called Mandy* mom.

Todd was on the phone calling in the emergency, his expertise obvious by the words he chose to explain the situation in a calm and precise manner. It seemed to take forever, but the ambulance arrived at the church within minutes.

Sophia watched as everyone hovered over Mandy. She'd made it a few steps closer to the scene. So this was Mandy, and she was pregnant. Tears stung her eyes, and hate filled her belly.

"Where are her papers?" Todd asked over the commotion.

"In her purse," David answered. Sophia felt sick.

"Where are her DNR papers and the papers we had her sign?"

"All in her purse." David repeated, holding tight to her hand. "The baby. Is the baby okay?" he asked the paramedics, and the words shot through Sophia. "You can't stop saving her until the baby is here."

A paramedic who wrote information on his gloved hand asked, "What's her name?"

"Mandy Kendal," David said.

Sophia swayed, but Mary Alice was there with her hands on her shoulders to steady her.

The paramedics lifted Mandy onto the gurney. She was hooked to monitors and had an IV, and Sophia wasn't sure how it had all gotten in place.

"The baby is fine. We'll get her there in time." They began to push her out. "Who's riding with us?"

"I am," David said, following them out of the hall.

"And who are you?"

"David Kendal. I'm the baby's father," he said clearly.

Sophia's legs gave out from under her and she sat down on the floor.

The hall emptied within minutes. Sophia remained on the floor with her head between her knees, trying to suck in what air she could. Mary Alice brought her a cup of water and sat down next to her.

"I'll take you to the hospital."

"Are you out of your mind? I'm not going there." Her stomach burned from the pain of deceit.

"You left last time without asking questions. Don't do it this time."

"Oh, you can bet I won't. I'll ask him questions until his dear lungs run out of breath answering them." She clenched her teeth, but a wave of emotion escaped in a grunt.

"Then listen when he does." There was no more tenderness in Mary Alice's voice.

"What do you know about all of this?"

"I don't know anything. But I know for a fact, no matter what that man said, that baby is not his."

"He admitted it in front of everyone. Of course it's his." Sophia's words were icy and bitter.

"I've been around for the past ten years. I've been the wife of his closest friend for that long. I'm the employer of his daughter. I stayed up nights drinking coffee and talking to him when you walked out and he was suddenly a father and didn't know what to do. I was the shoulder he cried on when Carissa was raked over the coals by the counselor at school when she wrecked her bike and they wouldn't leave her alone. I was there helping him clean up when Mandy lost her mind and tried to kill herself, and I've been here watching him pine his life away waiting for you. Where have *you* been?"

The air in the room was gone again, leaving her light-headed, and Sophia sobbed, but her tears had dried up.

She looked up and realized Mary Alice was still sitting there on the floor with her. Just like a best friend would.

She found tears again, and they fell. Katie handed her a napkin, and she wiped them away.

"Come on, I'll take you and the ladies home." Mary Alice stood and offered her hands to Sophia, who took them and rose to her feet.

"I love you. I'm so sorry…"

"I love you too, and that's why I'm not slapping you silly right now." Mary Alice wrapped her arms around Sophia and held her tight. "You're going to go home and get some rest. You look beat. I'll go down and see what I can find out." She held her at arm's length. "But he'll come to you, and you know he will. Listen when he talks. He's going to have one hell of a story to tell you."

The last two weeks had been a whirlwind. She'd really only spent four days with David. In all honesty, how could she expect that ten years would mend in four days?

She closed her eyes for a moment, but the image of David holding Mandy's hand had seared into her mind.

When the sun peeked through Sophia's bedroom window, she opened her eyes. It was a new day. A day Sophia had begun to doubt would ever arrive.

She dressed and slipped into her running shoes. A quick look outside confirmed David's car wasn't in the driveway. Not that she'd expected to see it there.

Pushing aside any thought of what he was going through, Sophia started down the stairs. She opened the front door and took in a breath of cool morning air. Her eyes ached from the night of tears she'd shed, and she shielded them from the sun.

"'Bout time," Katie said from her rocker. "Been waiting an hour for you."

"Grandma, it's only seven o'clock. What are you doing?" Her voice cracked.

"I figured you'd need to run. I didn't know if you'd do it with your shoes or with your suitcases, but I figured."

Sophia shook her head and let out a breath. She'd been pegged. "I thought a run would be nice. Clear my head."

Katie patted the seat of the chair next to her and waited till Sophia sat. "What are you going to do?"

"I don't know."

"Teaching position at the high school is going to open up next fall. Carissa said that old man is going to retire. That was after he told her he'd never heard anyone play that piece of music as lovely as she did."

"She got the chair?" Sophia felt a lift in the tension that resided in her neck, and she could swear she felt her heart swell with pride.

"She sure did," Katie said, patting Sophia's leg. "She was pretty happy, though she would have been much happier had you been here to share it with her."

Sophia's head dipped down. "Grandma, I've made such big mistakes, and I thought I could get past them. Now I don't know what to think." A tear welled in her eye, and she batted it away. "That woman had his last name and *he* said that was his baby. Todd Krantz seemed to know about it, too."

"Well I sure as hell don't know what's going on, but he'll tell us. He closed on that house he built the other day. I think they'll still look for one around here though, being that it's Carissa's last year and all." She sat quietly for a moment, resting her gaze on Sophia. "What about you. Are you staying?"

She swallowed the lump of fear that had lodged itself in her throat. "I want to. I just don't know if I can handle it."

"You can. You're a strong woman."

"I had thought about staying no matter what happened between me and David. I even looked at the house on Cherry Street. I put in a bid for it."

"Did you?"

Sophia nodded. "Carissa took me by it, and the realtor was there."

"Carissa? What did she think of the house?"

"I don't know. I didn't ask. She just figured I'd need a place to live if I stayed. They both want me to stay."

"I think he asked you to stay, get married, and be a mother."

Sophia nodded again. "But now…"

"David looked at the house too."

"Yes, I know."

"Still looked as nice as when you both lived there and fixed it up."

Sophia shot a look at her grandmother. "You went through the house too?" Katie nodded. "Why?"

"You know, this was supposed to be a much happier event."

"What are you talking about?"

Katie pulled a chain from around her neck. Dangling from it was a key. Sophia's eyes widened.

"I both lost the sale of the house." Sophia narrowed her eyes on her grandmother.

"Yes, and so did David. You were both pains in the ass when I was trying to close the deal." Katie grinned.

"Grandma, what did you do?"

Katie handed her the key. "I wanted you home. I bought back your home. This is my gift for you because you've always been such a wonderful gift to me."

The tears that had welled in her eyes fell. She scooted out of her chair, knelt before her grandmother, and wrapped her arms around her. "I don't know what to say."

"Say you'll stay in Kansas City for the rest of my life. Say no matter what happens, you'll be there for that girl who needs you. Say you'll never cover your scars again, and you'll be proud of who you are."

"Oh, Grandma." She wiped the tears that had begun rolling down her cheeks.

Katie lifted Sophia's chin. "Now say 'Goodbye, Grandma, I'm going home.'"

Sophia took the key from her grandmother's hand and held it to her chest.

"Goodbye, Grandma. I'm going home," she said and then sprinted off toward *her* house.

CHAPTER FOURTEEN

Sophia wasn't sure how fast she'd run, but she'd made it to the house in no time. She noticed the sign out front—SOLD! She smiled and ran up the steps. Waiting for her, just as promised, was a basket filled with grape jelly.

She turned to look across the street, where Mrs. Crow sat on her porch and waved. Sophia picked up the basket and waved back.

Taking the key from around her neck, she unlocked the door she'd unlocked so many times before and then walked inside. There she stood in the empty house. Her house. The house that was, and would be again, her home. Warmth washed over her like a blanket.

She moved through slowly, taking in each room as though she'd never seen it. She already had ideas of things to do in each room—new curtains in one, a coat of paint in another. Her mind was filling, and she was smiling again. She wished she had a paper and a pen to jot down her thoughts.

She spent the entire day in the empty house, reacquainting herself with everything she'd fallen in love with in the first place.

"You look like you're right at home." David's voice startled her, and she turned with a jerk to see him standing in the living room.

He wore the same clothes he'd had on at the party. His tie was missing, his shirt was untucked, and his hair bore tracks where his fingers had run through it over and over. He carried a white box and a picture frame.

"I forgot to give these to you earlier. I thought it would look good up here." He opened the box and set a little glass cello on the mantel. "The cello is from a gift shop in Hawaii. The card is in the box. When the man found out I knew you, he wanted you to have it."

He set the picture frame next to the glass cello and stepped back.

"I hope you don't mind I brought this back with me from Seattle."

Her eyes filled with tears. She pursed her lips as she batted away the tears.

Sophia studied the items and then turned to him. "How did you get in here?" Her words were angry, and her heart ached.

He held up the key.

"Oh, no. No, they did not."

"Yes, they did. *This* is our wedding present." But that wasn't what Katie had told her.

"Well then, I guess we should discuss it." She walked a step closer to him with her arms crossed over her chest. "Oh, wait. You already have a new house."

"Not one your daughter wants to live in."

Sophia clenched her jaw. "My daughter?"

"You asked Carissa to be your daughter. Remember? Right before you were going to ask me to be your husband."

"Well, I don't see that happening anymore."

"Why not?"

"Why not? Oh, David, you…" She turned from him, but he caught her arm and pulled her to him tight. "Let go."

"No. Not till you tell me your answer."

"My answer?"

"Yes. Will you marry me?" His touch was soft and gentle when he lifted his hand to her cheek and back into her hair.

"Do you really expect me to marry you now?" She trembled on the verge of a complete breakdown.

"Yes."

"David, let me go."

"You said you loved me. You said you trusted me, and that you'd stand behind any decisions I made."

"That was before you left in the back of an ambulance with a pregnant woman that you'd sworn was out of your life. Oh, and after you told them that it was your baby and her last name is Kendal. What did I miss, David? I wasn't in Rome that long."

"Will you marry me?"

"Go to hell." She pushed up her arms, broke free of him, and bolted for the stairs.

"Do you want to hear my story," he called, "or are you going to run again?"

His words stopped her, but she didn't face him. She couldn't face him.

He walked toward her.

"There's more to lose than just me now, Sophie. I have baggage, and I'm proud of it." When she didn't turn to face him, he came around her, his eyes blazing. "Carissa needs you. You offered her what she has always wanted. Are you going to walk out on her?"

She wondered if he'd rehearsed his words to cut her as they did.

"She has a mother." Sophia spit out the words.

"No, Sophie." His voice dropped. "We lost her."

His face was somber, but tired. Dark circles around his eyes made it evident that he hadn't slept.

"David, I'm sorry."

"It was what she wanted." He held out his hand to offer her a seat on the stairs, and she sat. She had promised Mary Alice she would listen to him. He took her hand and twisted the ring on her finger between his fingers. "You didn't take this off."

"I was waiting to see you. I wanted to throw it in your face."

"I'm glad you didn't." He raised her fingers to his lips and gently held them there. "May I explain?"

Numbly, she nodded.

His words washed over her. *Changed her name…affair…weak heart…knew she was going to die.*

She covered her mouth with her free hand. She would have thought she'd run out of tears by now, but they continued to fall. David brushed them away.

"They kept her alive long enough for the baby to be born, and then she was gone. Her heart gave out, just as she told me it would. She never even got to see Hope." He choked on his own words.

"Hope?"

"Carissa named her. She thought it was what the baby deserved. Hope."

"That's…beautiful," she choked through her tears.

He cupped her face with his hands and looked into her eyes. "As of yesterday at five twenty-three, I am the father of a beautiful five-pound, three-ounce baby girl."

Sophia stood and turned from him. Her heart ached, and her stomach churned.

"I wanted to tell you, Sophie." His voice was ragged. "After Carissa and I discussed it, I wanted to tell you, but you were gone." David stood and rested his hands on her shoulders. "I did this for Carissa. She asked me to. She couldn't bear to have her sister shipped off to someone she didn't know." He took her tears from her cheeks with his thumbs. "Sophie, I did this for you too. For us."

"What? How is this for us?"

"I wanted Hope to be yours. A baby of your own."

Her heart hammered in her chest. He couldn't actually have thought she'd just accept something like that.

"You knew about the baby before I left, didn't you?" she asked, remembering him talking about babies landing on doorsteps.

He swallowed hard. "Yes."

The room seemed to dissolve and swirl around her as the truth of what he'd done sank in.

Well, wasn't that what she'd prayed for? Didn't she want to marry David and have a baby dropped on the doorstep? And hadn't she even wanted that doorstep to be the one on Cherry Street?

David hunched his shoulders. "I'd understand if you wanted to leave me and never speak to me again. I had to do what I did in a short amount of time. But either way, I have a baby to take care of now, and to tell you the truth, I'm scared to death." He released a slow breath. "I'm prepared to let you go if I have to, but, Sophie, I don't want to." He reached into his breast pocket and pulled out a picture. He handed it to her.

She gazed at the newborn and wiped frantically at her tears, which flowed freely.

"I'll let you be alone for a little while. I've just given you a lot to think about. We'll stay at the new house. Call me."

David turned to leave the house. He kept walking until she called out his name.

"Is she healthy?"

"Yes. She's in intensive care right now. She's pretty little. She'll be there for a few weeks because she was early, and they need her to be a little bigger. They also need to make sure everything is okay before they send her home. Mandy's body gave out before she was born, and that caused some trauma. But she's fine." His eyes beamed with love when he spoke of her. "Mandy really was clean and sober for the last few years, and that Hope is doing so well proves it."

She didn't want to know anything about the woman who'd come between her and David and destroyed their relationship once—maybe twice. But the compassion in his eyes made her ask.

"What changed her?"

"I don't know. Somewhere in her life she had a change of heart about things. She knew she couldn't do right by her new baby, but she knew her baby deserved to have a good home." He stepped closer. "She said you'd be a good mother."

Sophia stared down at the picture of the baby. Every emotion she'd ever known twisted inside of her. She was angry with David, mourning for a woman she'd grown to hate, and elated that he wanted to share the gift of a child with her. How could everything she'd ever wanted come with such a price?

"David, this is a lot to think about."

"I know it is." He moved even closer, but he didn't touch her. "Listen, take your time. If you've accepted the house from your grandmother, that means you're staying." He looked at her for validation, and when she nodded, he looked relieved. "I've done what I've done, and there's no going back. And I don't want to. Carissa is in love with Hope, and so am I."

He gathered her hands in his. "I want to share this with you, Sophie. I want this to be *our* gift." He kissed her fingers and released her. "If I can only have your friendship, I'd settle for that. Right now, I sure could use a friend."

Sophia nodded, but remained silent for a few moments and tried to process it all. She closed her eyes and sucked in a deep breath of courage. She was a warrior. She was a survivor.

She opened her eyes to see David's weary ones looking back at her. He was offering her everything she'd ever wanted. How could she not take it and move on? After all, her trip home was supposed to be about her moving on to the next part in her life. Two weeks ago, though, she never would have imagined it would have included a house, a husband, and two daughters.

She took a deep breath.

"Can I meet her? Can I meet Hope?"

His eyes opened wider, and his lips curled into a soft smile.

"Of course. Carissa is with her now. She can't get enough of her." He angled his head. "Are you sure?"

Her stomach flipped, and she nodded. "I think I should see my daughter. My daughters."

"Do you mean that?"

Sophia nodded. "I wouldn't want sisters separated any more than I want to be separated from you."

"One more time, Sophie. Will you marry me?"

"Yes, I will marry you."

"And we'll raise a family, right here in *our* house?"

She nodded, rose on her toes, and wrapped her arms around his neck. "Just like we'd always planned to do." She pressed a gentle kiss to his lips and let it linger. He pulled her tighter and she deepened the kiss, letting the mistakes of the past dissolve around them and the joy of new things to come envelop them.

"You do know those crazy, old women conned Carissa into helping them," he said, resting his forehead against hers.

"Matchmaking again?" She kissed him again. "Well, we don't want to let them down."

I hope you enjoyed book 1 in the Matchmaker series.
Please enjoy an excerpt from book 2
Encore
Releasing July 2013

Chapter One

Her young student pulled the bow across the strings of the violin and the sound was pure evil. Carissa Kendal winced, and then quickly smiled. She'd get it in time. Eventually, they all got it if they stuck around.

The dropout rate of students was the one dark cloud over her next venture, the Kendal School of Music. It had been her dream to teach music in her own school and she was about to dive into it. She'd hoped her mother would want to be by her side more, but Sophia still had Hope to raise. Carissa accepted that, but to have her mother call up an old friend to help her wasn't settling.

Did Sophia not think she'd look him up? That she wouldn't find out who he was?

At the moment, he was nobody. Every musical endeavor he'd pursued in the eight years since renowned tenor Pablo DiAngelo's ensemble broke up had failed spectacularly.

Why was Sophia soft on him? Her mother's name carried far more influence than that of the failed pianist, and would have given Carissa's music school all the prestige it needed.

The student pulled another evil note and snapped Carissa from her thoughts.

"I'm never going to get this," the young girl complained with her nose wrinkled.

"You will. If you want to, you'll get it." She smiled encouragingly, remembering when she'd been that young girl. "You need to remember to practice the material I give you." Carissa raised her eyebrows with the subtle demand.

"Okay. I promise I'll be better next time."

"And if you practice, that will always be the case."

As her student gathered her instrument, Carissa marked off her lesson sheet and handed it to her.

They left the study of the old boardinghouse, where Carissa lived with her grandmother, and stood by the door as her student's mother walked toward them. Carissa gave the girl a squeeze on her shoulder.

"She's doing wonderfully. A little extra practice each day will help," she said. "Don't forget your peppermint on your way out the door."

The young girl fished in the bowl for the right piece of candy as Carissa opened the front door. The violinist's mother handed Carissa a check for the lesson.

"Thank you, Carissa. She enjoys her lessons very much."

"I'm pleased to hear that. We'll see you both next week."

As the woman and her daughter descend the front steps, a man paid a cab on the street in front of the old house. He stood with his suitcase in his hand and looked her way.

He was tall, too thin for her taste, but he looked almost regal in the way he carried himself. He removed his sunglasses and stroked the wisps of dirty blond hair from his eyes. She almost didn't recognize the man from the pictures she'd seen on the Internet.

He looked like a blond Jimmy Stewart, and her stomach did a little flip.

"Hello," he called as he neared the house. She smiled despite her misgivings. He even walked like Jimmy Stewart.

Like most of Pablo's ensemble, he'd always walked behind the man with the million-dollar smile, never next to or in front of, not like her mother who had been paraded on Pablo's arm. It was no wonder she hadn't recognized him.

She extended her hand to him, and as his fingers enclosed hers, she gulped in air. He was strikingly handsome. She hadn't expected that.

To have played for Pablo, as Sophia had, Thomas had to be tremendously talented. Yet would the curse that hung over his career affect her music school?

"You must be Thomas Samuel. I'm Sophia's daughter, Carissa Kendal. I've heard a lot about you."

When Sophia Kendal had said her daughter would meet him at the boardinghouse in Kansas City, he hadn't expected she'd look like the woman standing before him. The woman before him stood erect as a dancer. Her hair fell to the middle of her back like an ebony waterfall, and her dark eyes were soft. She wore a flowing orange blouse and a long skirt of the same orange, mixed with earthy browns that swirled around her calves when she moved.

She was mesmerizing.

"Please come in." She stepped back through the door. Heat rose on the back of his neck as he passed by her. "My mother says you'll be staying with us until you get settled."

"Uh. Yes." He felt like his tongue had swollen. "I'm sorry if I seem out of sorts. I knew Sophia for so long, to think of her as your mother, well, that's a stretch for me."

Carissa smiled at him again. "I was seventeen before she adopted me, so I can understand. I'm sorry you couldn't make it out for their wedding."

"Yes, so am I." Had he made that wedding, he'd have made it his business to become more familiar with the dark beauty who, with the most subtle gesture of tucking her hair behind her ear, had his pulse climbing.

Guilt halted his thoughts. He should have been at the wedding because he'd promised Sophia he would be. It was just another broken promise, and he feared he would let her down again. And given his past, he had no business fantasizing about Carissa—or any woman. It could end only in heartache. Or worse.

"So you're a teacher?"

"Yes. That's my dream, to bring music to the masses through their own fingers."

"You play the cello, right? Just like your mother?"

"Yes. Even before I met her she was my inspiration."

"Why are you only giving lessons? Why aren't you in the symphony?" From what he knew, Carissa's talent was as superior as her mother's.

"I'm a caregiver. My mother needed to look after my little sister, and I chose to take care of the women who took care of me growing up." Her dark eyes clouded with sadness. "My aunt Millie had cancer, and we lost her about six years ago."

"I'm so sorry." He fought the urge to reach out to her.

"Thank you. But now I'm taking care of my grandmother, who will be ninety-two soon."

"She lives here? With you?"

Carissa nodded. "Well, I live with her. But yes, and she's still feisty as ever."

"I heard that," an elderly woman called as she walked from the kitchen, slowly, balancing with a walker.

"Katie," Carissa said, "this is Mr. Samuel. The man mom sent over."

"Mr. Samuel, it's nice to meet you." He shook her hand with a gentle grasp. "Thank you. And please call me Thomas."

"All right, I will." She turned to Carissa. "I'm going to go lie down. Get Thomas settled. I think your parents will be over soon for dinner. Wake me when they arrive."

Thomas" belly clutched. Sophia and David were coming for dinner. Suddenly he felt dizzy. He hadn't sat down to a meal with a family in a very long time. It shouldn't bother him; this was Sophia, after all. He'd spent plenty of time with Sophia.

What would she think of him now? Now that he was washed up, broke, and had failed at everything he had always hoped he'd accomplish.

Carissa kissed her grandmother on the cheek. Thomas watched the exchange. He'd known them both but moments, yet he knew what they meant to each other. He was envious.

"Thank you again, Mrs. Burkhalter, for letting me stay here with you."

"You can stay as long as you call me Katie." She gave him a stern nod.

"Yes, ma'am, Katie."

Katie made her way down the hall to a bedroom, and shut the door behind her.

"Wow." He shook his head. "I feel like I've just met a legend. For years I heard about Sophia's grandmother. I feel like I've known her forever."

"Next to my mother she's one of the most amazing women to me." Carissa's eyes followed the path her grandmother had walked, her devotion to the older woman glistening in her expression. "Why don't I show you to your room and you can get some rest before dinner." She turned back to him, catching his stare. "I'm sure it was a long flight from Rome."

"Yes it was." Too long. Every minute of the flight he'd fought with himself over whether it'd been right to accept Sophia's job offer. He followed Carissa up the stairs.

The room was as large as his apartment in Rome, yet more homey. It had a brass bed that looked as old as the house. Two chairs sat on either side of the window with a marble-topped table between them. A door stood ajar, revealing an adjoining bathroom, so he wouldn't need to share facilities with others in the house.

The room felt masculine and that pleased him. He'd been worried about staying in the house of an old woman, with doilies under everything and untouchable collectables, and had almost called a hotel and made reservations. He was glad he hadn't.

"This room was my father's while we lived here. I think you should find it suiting." Carissa pushed back the sheers, and the afternoon light filled the room.

"I think this will be wonderful."

"Good." She pushed open the bathroom door. "Your bathroom is through here. It adjoins to the other room, but no one uses that room anymore."

"Anymore?"

She let out a laugh that was as mesmerizing as her looks. "That was my room, on the other side. When I moved back in to take care of my grandmother and aunt, I took my mother's old room. It was her room growing up. It's really big and has its own bathroom." The smile that danced on her face was childlike. "So if you need anything, I'm just down the hall."

Her innocent offer punched him in the gut. He only nodded as he watched her leave. He already knew he'd be in need of her. And because he couldn't allow himself to have her, his nights here would be miserable.

He forced himself to focus on Sophia's school. An entire school dedicated to bringing music to children. Too many school districts had ripped it out of schools because of funding. The idea was stellar! Her request for his help in putting it together had sent his dragging self-esteem through the roof. It hadn't taken but a week to pack his few belongings and board the one-way flight to America to start a new chapter in his life right there in Kansas City,

Missouri.

He had learned so much from Sophia when he'd started playing with Pablo. To work with her on something as great as a school made his heart pound.

There was a snag, of course. Carissa Kendal would assuredly be one of the teachers.

He squeezed his eyes shut and pushed away the thought. He wasn't looking for a woman. He wasn't looking for the complications of a relationship. He didn't come from the kind of family that embraced love and commitment. That, he knew, had to run deep enough to run through one's blood. Thomas Samuel was an amazing musician and composer—but lover, husband, or father material? He'd never know. He'd never bring a woman into his circle and hurt her like that. Because that's what he'd do. He'd hurt her, just as his father had hurt the ones he was supposed to love.

He blew out a breath. They had a lot in common, the members of Pablo's ensemble. Pablo had run from whom he was. Sophia had run from what she thought. Thomas had run from what he might become.

He'd run for a long time. He'd left the States when he was only seventeen and started touring with Pablo almost immediately. He'd been Pablo's prodigy. Far away from his family, if you could call it that.

His family didn't live too far from where he stood questioning his very being. Fear fluttered in his heart. Occasionally he let himself dream of being part of a family again, but he knew it could never come true.

As it was, he was going to wash up, go downstairs, and dine with Sophia's family. A family he already knew a great deal about. But the nerves wouldn't subside. They were a family and he was an outsider, just as he'd always been. A commotion filtered through the house, and Thomas followed the sound toward the wonderfully large kitchen. With her back turned to him, Carissa stood at the sink beside her mother. Heat rushed through him.

They were laughing, joking, and bumping into each other over the sink.

"If you'd move your big behind…" Sophia directed the insult to Carissa.

"Oh, excuse me, Miss-I-Haven't-Seen-a-Treadmill-in-a-Year." Carissa boosted back and they both laughed.

He could see that happiness had landed on Sophia. She'd always been a firm and taut person, but the few pounds that had crept onto her let him know she was truly joyous in her role of wife and mother.

"Who are you?" a small voice asked from the table.

The laughter died and Thomas turned his head to the table, where Katie sat. A young girl with rosy cheeks, deep blue eyes, and mounds of blonde curls sat next to Katie, looking up at him. He smiled cautiously at her.

"I'm Thomas, who are you?"

"I'm Hope. I'm eight." Her expression clearly said, you should have known that.

"Thomas!" Sophia squealed as she grabbed for a towel to wipe her hands on and then she raced across the room and wrapped her arms around him.

He breathed her in.

She pulled him back at arm's length to study him and he did the same. Her auburn hair was a bit longer, but her brown eyes were just as welcoming. When she smiled at him, he knew he'd found a home. One thing about Sophia, she could always make him feel at home.

"I can't believe you're here. I can't believe you're standing right here." Tears formed in her eyes and she pulled him to her again. He held him tight. Already he was glad he'd come.

"How come there is some man hugging my wife in the kitchen and you are all standing around watching?" Thomas stiffened at the sound of the man's voice.

"Daddy!" Hope ran into the man's arms and embraced him. Still in his pilot's uniform, he bent down to hug his daughter. "This is Thomas. He knows Mommy."

"Well, maybe you should introduce us."

Hope nodded and walked her father by the hand to Thomas, who still held one arm around Sophia.

"Daddy, this is Thomas."

"Thomas, it's nice to meet you. I'm David Kendal." He extended his hand and Thomas shook it.

"It's an honor to meet you. I feel like I know you very well."

"Considering the time frame in which you got your stories, I'd beg for another chance to make a first impression." He touched his wife's cheek and she moved forward and kissed him gently.

"Mr. Kendal, she never had a bad word to say about you." He looked at Sophia.

"She should have come home sooner, then."

"You know, I'm not going to stand here and relive the fact I made a mistake years ago." Sophia threw up her hands and shook her head with a smile. "Is there anyone in this kitchen who doesn't think I'm a wonderful granddaughter, mother, friend, and wife?"

They shook their heads.

"Okay, then, everything ended well and we can eat."

Thomas found himself seated between Hope and Carissa at the dinner table. If he let himself look at Carissa, he was sure he'd end up tripping over his tongue like a lovesick puppy, so he made an effort to take an interest in her younger sister. One look at Hope and he saw similarities to Carissa, though Hope was fair and Carissa's complexion darker. The resemblance was amazing for an adopted child.

Katie passed the salad bowl over the top of Hope, who wrinkled her nose. With a nod from Katie, Thomas dropped a small spoonful onto her plate, and Katie smiled. She reminded him a little of his own grandmother.

"So, Thomas, you're a pianist?"

"Yes, ma'am. I've been playing piano since I was three."

"That's awfully young."

"Well, my grandmother insisted and she taught me my very first scales." The memory was one of the few from his childhood that could bring a smile to his face.

"Wise woman."

David passed a plate of roast to Katie. "So are you sure you're up to helping these two with their school? They can be awfully demanding."

"I can't tell you how excited I was to get Sophia's call. What's happening with music programs in schools is pitiful. It doesn't make sense to take the arts away. When you start doing that…" All eyes were on him and he realized he was about to go on a rant. "Well, I think it's foolish, and bringing music to others is what I do best."

He felt Carissa's eyes on him and he turned to catch her stare. Her cheeks flushed immediately and then she turned away. He sucked in a breath and lifted his water glass to his lips to try to cool off his racing mind.

Carissa dipped her head toward her plate and buttered her roll. He believed in the cause. Yes, that was what She'd wanted. She wasn't sure he'd have understood the mission. After all he was a down-and-out performer and she was a teacher.

And she'd been so conflicted with her mother's idea of bringing Thomas into their school. And now that he was here all she could think about was him, not as a musician or teacher, but as a man. A man whose passion for sharing the gift of music she found more than attractive.

She took a bite of her roast. Did Thomas feel the heat between them or was that just her?

His hypnotic blue eyes and that disheveled sandy hair that he kept running his fingers through had her heart fluttering. Heat prickled her skin, and that mortified her. She'd felt like this before, just not over someone She'd barely met. And she'd been burned before. This time she wasn't going to jump straight into bed with a guy just because he was hot.

"Don't you think so, Carissa?" her father asked and she darted her head up.

"I'm sorry, what?"

"Don't you think that school will be operational by the time the schools return from their winter break?" he repeated.

"Oh, yes." She blew out a small breath. "We took possession of the building two days ago. There is a lot of work to be done and that should take us through December." Thomas's eyes were on her and she took the courage to look at him and finish, calm and professional— the way their relationship would be. "We'll start enrollment in the first part of December. We've talked to the local schools about passing out our information and doing some assemblies for the students. I think we should be able to reach a lot of kids."

"You've already done a lot of work to ensure your success." He shifted his eyes to her mother. "Sophia, I'm so impressed."

"Well, I'm just the silent partner. This was really all Carissa's doing. This is her dream." Carissa smiled as her mother laid a gentle hand on hers.

She leveled her eyes with Thomas's as he turned back to her. That intoxicating blue peered into her soul and she felt her heart hitch. Against her will, the corners of her mouth turned up into a smile. He grinned at her, melting her resolve.

"Thank you for considering me for your staff, then. It is going to be an honor to work with you."

That was it. Her heart was gone.

All she had to do was keep Thomas from finding out.

Meet the Author

Bernadette Marie has been an avid writer since the early age of 13, when she'd fill notebook after notebook with stories that she'd share with her friends. Her journey into novel writing started the summer before eighth grade when her father gave her an old typewriter. At all times of the day and night you would find her on the back porch penning her first work, which she would continue to write for the next 22 years.

In 2007—after marriage, filling her chronic entrepreneurial needs, and having five children—Bernadette began to write seriously with the goal of being published. That year she wrote 12 books. In 2009 she was contracted for her first trilogy and the published author was born. In 2011 she (being the entrepreneur that she is) opened her own publishing house, 5 Prince Publishing, and has released her own contemporary titles. She also quickly began the process of taking on other authors in other genres.

In 2012 Bernadette Marie began to find herself on the bestsellers lists of iTunes, Amazon, and Barnes and Noble to name a few. Her office wall is lined with colorful PostIt notes with the titles of books she will be releasing in the very near future, with hope that they too will grace the bestsellers lists.

Bernadette spends most of her free time driving her kids to their many events—usually hockey. She is also an accomplished martial artist with a second degree black belt in Tang Soo Do. An avid reader, she enjoys contemporary romances with humor and happily ever afters.

Other titles published by
www.5princebooks.com